PREHISTORI(
THE GRAVI

CW01507582

Table of Contents

CHAPTER 1 | SOMETHING AMISS 1

CHAPTER 2 | MONSTER IN THE WALLS 9

CHAPTER 3 | THE OLD CODGER............................ 19

CHAPTER 4 | DATE WITH A DINOSAUR............. 27

CHAPTER 5 | THE HORROR HALLWAY 35

CHAPTER 6 | THE RADIO 45

CHAPTER 7 | GREG AND LYDIA............................ 55

CHAPTER 8 | TWO LOST LOVERS..................... 65

CHAPTER 9 | SMALL BUT DEADLY 75

CHAPTER 10 | ARMED AND DANGEROUS 83

CHAPTER 11 | A DANCE WITH HADES 91

CHAPTER 12 | UGLY TRUTH 103

Time to Scream | TRESPASSID 115

Crow's Vengeance | CAWS OF DEATH 121

CHAPTER 1

SOMETHING AMISS

"Ah, good ole nightshift," moaned Bruce as he placed his bag of essentials; pot noodles, crisps and coffee onto the X-ray baggage scanner - the same ones you'd find at an airport.

Bruce Cooper was a tall, bald man with considerable mass about him. Some might call him a bear, others a boar. His gut *did* push against his shirt seams, threatening all those daring to look with a button to the face. Yet, his size suited him. It made him appear strong and complimented his Viking-style ginger beard.

"ID please," requested Tony, the officer controlling the scanner. He was a young man, around thirty, with petite features and thinning hair; the latter was an indicator that he'd served five years of stressful service. But less than ten, of course, because he still made an effort with his uniform. His white shirt and black formal trousers were crisply ironed; including the 'HMP' epaulettes on his shoulders; his boots were clean *and shiny*; and his black tie sat perfectly straight.

Bruce laughed as he wiped fluff from his own creased, two-day-old shirt. "Really, Tony?"

They never asked him for his ID, nobody did, not anymore. He'd worked here for thirteen years. Everybody knew him.

"Come on Bruce, it's the rules. You know this. ID please."

Bruce laughed again. "Did your crystal ball arrive recently?"

"My crystal ball?" replied Tony, puzzled.

"Yeah, well you must be a psychic or something because you knew my name without my ID. It's like you already identified me."

"W-well," replied the young man, flustered. "I still need to see it."

Bruce waved him rudely and ignored the request. He walked through the metal detector, again like those at an airport. He did not care that it lit up and bleeped, and continued to walk, waiting for his bag to come through the scanner.

"You set off the detector. Do you have metal on you?"

"It's my boots," declared Bruce.

"I need them off please and through the X-ray. I need to check them."

"They always bleep, you know this. It's always my boots."

"Bruce," commanded Tony sternly, darting his eyes across the lobby.

Bruce looked to where he was looking and saw two unfamiliar managers quietly conversing with a third – his night shift manager. All three were recognisable by the two stars on their shoulder epaulettes.

The lobby itself was surprisingly welcoming, like a hotel reception.

An electronically controlled door, requiring fingerprint access, led to the security area where Bruce stood. This itself was simple; narrow, to control footfall. To the left was a wooden desk, modern, where Tony stood controlling the X-ray. Past the metal detector was a key fob-operated barrier and beyond that was a large area with seating for visitors, where the managers stood. These blue padded seats were expensive, comfortable. Another electronically controlled door stood at the opposite end allowing access to the prison's main grounds.

And yet, the intimidation such security measures might have brought was masked by bright colourful paint, immaculately cleaned floors and posters depicting success stories; shadowing the misery defining the rest of the prison. There was even a trophy cabinet.

"Ah," laughed Bruce, as he watched the managers curiously. He pulled out his ID card, of a much younger self *with hair*, and took off his boots. "Sorry for being a grump, didn't get much sleep last night."

Tony chuckled. "You must not sleep any night then."

"Ha. Ha," grinned Bruce as he glanced at them again. "So what are they in for? Are they headquarters managers? Did somebody die in custody? Somebody important?"

"They *are* from headquarters, yeah, but I have no idea why they're here," said Tony with a shrug. "Seems serious though. They've been chatting for quite a while. Even had the Governor on the phone, there were talks about her coming in for the night too."

One of the managers noticed Bruce put his boots back on and walked over with great prowess, like a lion commanding his jungle. It would have been intimidating if the scrawny manager wasn't five foot tall and built like a matchstick.

"Have you got your baton tonight?" he asked in his squeaky voice which was rather fitting for his meagre physique.

"No?" scoffed Bruce. "It's the night shift."

"I'm well aware of what shift it is," the manager replied bluntly.

"So what do I need it for? The seagulls?"

"Go and get your baton from your locker," he said, flicking his eyebrow. *"Now."*

"It's optional," contested Bruce. He wasn't wrong either, he wasn't obligated to carry it. No one was.

"Are you arguing with a manager?"

Bruce grunted with a heavy sigh. He knew he wouldn't win this battle. And he was too drained to try. What *did* he need a baton for on the night shift though? The doors were all locked, the prisoners inside. There hadn't been an escape in fifty years, and he'd be confident for the next fifty. In truth, he didn't mind carrying it. He usually did. He was just very tired tonight and had forgotten. *In truth,* he couldn't be bothered walking back to his locker. He hadn't indulged in an essential coffee yet, which meant energy was lacking. And motivation scarcer.

Despite such, he returned through security, teased by embers from Tony's warm brew animating the air. He placed his finger on the scanner to the noise of the door unlocking; confirming he was not a prisoner, and exited the lobby into the vestibule area.

To his right were glass revolving doors exiting the prison into the car park. Ahead of him was a desk where an officer usually sat to welcome visitors. And to his left was a key-fob-operated door leading to the staff facilities.

He made for his left, through the door, up a set of stairs and through various corridors leading to numerous amenities; canteen, gym, recreation rooms. He eventually reached the locker area - rows and rows of tiny lockers which serviced the prison's massive staffing.

Bruce opened his locker, quickly using the opportunity to check his phone as it wasn't allowed past security. Poor connection as always, but a notification from a news article trickled through. It piqued his interest; "*Tragic Experiment Gone Wrong – Lock Your Doors Tonight.*"

Tragic Experiment? He tried clicking the link but with bitter luck. His phone returned a white page, taunting him. He turned flight mode on and off. He even tried connecting to the staff Wi-Fi. Nothing. Nothing worked.

'Ah well,' he thought, shrugging. He'd best not waste any more time.

He flinched.

There was a shuffle nearby,

behind him.

He jumped,

almost dropping his phone.

And then there was a growl.

A low, menacing growl from something that was beyond hungry; something ravenous.

It caused Bruce's heart to skip a beat.

One.

Two.

Five seconds passed.

He approached cautiously, towards the noise, heart pounding in his puffed-out chest.

And then he chuckled.

The vending machine. The old machine hummed away, clunking every few seconds. It sounded horrible, age doing it no favours. And indeed, it was hungry, it needed filling. Like his own growling stomach.

'I really am tired tonight', chuckled Bruce to himself. He swapped his phone for his baton; a foot long of extendable metal and ventured back towards the lobby.

"Eh Bruce," said Tony, as Bruce bypassed both the metal detector and X-ray scanner. "I need your stuff back in the scanner. And your boots off again."

Bruce rolled his eyes but knew there was no point in arguing. The scrawny manager stared at him with prying eyes, just waiting for a reason to scold him.

"One baton secured," noted Bruce as he cleared security and approached the manager. There was slight ice to his tone, admittedly a tad disrespectful, as he waved it like a prized artefact. But again, he *was* grumpy without coffee in his veins.

"Good boy," replied the manager with a patronising tone as he tapped Bruce's shoulder and made to leave.

The second HQ manager looked worried, troubled even, as he followed quickly behind. It was as if he'd been given some grave news. The kind of news that caused your stomach to churn uncomfortably.

He stopped and turned towards Bruce. "Be vigilant tonight, okay? Keep safe."

"Roger that Sir, I'll be sure to stay away from any spiders," replied Bruce with a mocking salute. "And watch out for those speed bumps in the car park on the way out, they can be pretty vicious too."

The manager nodded, but didn't entertain Bruce's humour. The discomfort on his face had stolen his entire expression. He even sulked as he walked.

"What was all that about?" Bruce asked his own manager, Chris, as the other two, and Tony, each scanned their fingers and exited the lobby into the vestibule.

"It's eh," sighed Chris. "It's w-well. It's ah... Eh."

He couldn't seem to find his words. And yet, Chris Davidson never choked on his words. At six foot tall, boasting a chiselled jaw, perfect hairline and arms that were actually muscly, Chris demanded obedience simply by his presence. For his own voice to disobey his command, well: such was unusual.

"Spit it out, Captain America," jested Bruce.

"They were making sure our security was airtight," he said as he dimmed the lobby lights from a button on the security desk. He grabbed a set of keys which he'd use to lock the outside glass doors once the remaining staff, in this case the managers and Tony, had been to their lockers and left.

"At this time of night?" asked Bruce, confused. "And for what? No one's ever escaped."

Chris shook his head. He looked just as spooked as the second headquarters manager if not more. Just as uncomfortable too, as though he didn't want to be here. As if his own skin caused him to itch. Even the way he picked up the keys, hesitantly, twiddling them between his fingers... it was as though he didn't want to lock up.

"Not for escaping," wheezed Chris, almost screeching. "For getting in... *in case something got in.*"

CHAPTER 2
MONSTER IN THE WALLS

F or getting in...

The words repeated over and over in Bruce's head as he walked his first outside patrol of the night; a patrol of the prison's inner perimeter. Who'd be getting in? Why would anybody want in? It was a prison: hardly a pitstop for a good night. He chuckled - even he didn't enjoy being here and he was paid to be.

Chris unfortunately said nought on the matter, little in general actually. He'd sent Bruce on his first patrol earlier than normal, and alone. They'd always have a coffee first, and then do the patrol together. But not tonight. Something was amiss, something was unsettling. And that was enough to make Bruce feel uneasy too. He didn't like change to the status quo, especially when he was left in the dark. The literal dark.

For getting in?

Bruce looked at the perimeter as he walked past. Metal fencing stood around twelve feet tall with rugged, razor wire decorating the top. No person was getting over that. And that's presuming any intruder could climb the fifteen-foot concrete wall a few meters behind that, again boasting the same razor welcome.

The wind whistled through the menacing wire, screaming for its next victim. It would rip anything to shreds without mercy - anybody stupid enough to dare climb it. Even just looking at its sinister sharpness was enough to water Bruce's eyes.

Bruce extended his baton with a mighty swing, doubling its size, and smashed it against the fence as hard as he could, testing the sensors.

"Tango-Zulu-Five-Eight to Control Room message, over," he said through his radio. It was a standard radio for the prison service and looked both like a walkie-talkie and an old 'brick' style mobile phone with a long antenna.

"Send your message Tango-Zulu-Five-Eight, over."

"Commencing an alarm check on fence seventeen, over."

"Alarm triggered Bruce, fence secure."

"Received," replied Bruce, feeling a minuscule amount of reassurance that nobody was getting in tonight. Everything was as it should be, as it always was.

Yes, he thought. Nobody was getting in. Not tonight, not ever.

And yet, like a parasite in his brain, there was this nagging feeling he couldn't shake. The managers were concerned about something. Too concerned to set Bruce's mind at ease. It left a pointy stone in the pit of his stomach, a discomfort which he could not shake.

His brain flickered to images of a helicopter. That could work, he supposed. But why? 'Why would a helicopter land here?' he thought. That would take a lot of clout, a lot of resource. It wouldn't be worth the effort. HMP Kirkwood didn't hold notable prisoners worth breaking out; it was only a tiny jail in the north of Scotland. Murderers, sex offenders, petty thieves; all types of prisoners sure, but nobody infamous. There was no Jeffrey Dahmer in HMP Kirkwood.

He looked at the baton in his hand and laughed before putting it back into his baton pocket on the side of his trousers. He fantasised throwing it like a frisbee, like Thor would his hammer, towards the blades of any intruding helicopter. It would fall at his wrath. What a hero he'd be, he imagined. Bruce the Savior. He'd be Governor of his very own prison.

He chuckled at the thoughts. In the quiet boredom of the night shift – imagination was his friend.

He chuckled again. *Nobody was getting in*. He thought himself silly for even entertaining it. He worked in a prison. *A prison*. He was paid to stop people getting out, not in.

And so, he continued with his patrol which took around an hour. He made sure all doors and gates were locked and secure; making sure anything which could open, wasn't. He was also on the lookout for contraband-filled parcels that might have been thrown over from the outside, taking an extra second or two in the exercise yards. He kicked any rubbish, anything suspicious, that could hold phones, drugs, weapons - anything that an eager prisoner might be waiting to pick up in the morning.

As he came to the final quarter of his patrol, where there were more broken lights surrounding the perimeter than those working, he noticed how dark it suddenly was. The sun had slipped into its slumber, letting the moon take podium for the night. And yet still, it seemed darker than usual. Eerie even.

A heavy fog had set, thicker than expected. It was so thick he could taste it; he could taste salt, seaweed and rust from the sea nearby. It diluted the little light there was, reducing his vision. He normally didn't care about the dark, but it seeped through his skin causing an anxious sweat. Maybe it was his earlier unease, but it set his imagination into overdrive.

He quickened his steps subconsciously as the hairs on his entire body stood on end. They pulled at his skin as if they could sense something, something dangerous. Even the bricked prison buildings, the blocks, that he had walked past a million times before sent shivers down his spine.

The four-storey blocks, with caged windows, appeared a hundred feet tall, towering over him, suffocating him. Similarly, the enormous wall stood taller than usual, threatening to choke him dead. The cold, melancholic exterior ate at his soul piece by piece as it forced him into shadows darker than the night itself. And then there was the harrowing wire on top, like a poisoned cherry - it appeared like haunted trees from a nightmarish forest waiting to grab him at the earliest opportunity.

And it was endless.

No matter how many steps he took, both the buildings and exterior seemed to go on forever. Both seemed to twist in his mind and grow, becoming more frightening by the second. Shaping themselves into giants, monsters, ready to strike him down. It made him feel claustrophobic, caged; like *he* was the prisoner. Like he had nowhere to go.

His feet quickened still.

For getting in!

The words echoed in his head again, killing his earlier reassurances. Why was he afraid? Why now? Why was he thinking about this? Why did he need his baton? What did they know? What were they not telling him? Why was he alone? Was this a trap? Is he about to be ambushed? Is he about to die? Worse? *Are* the doors locked? *Is* everyone inside?

Nobody's getting in, he tried to tell himself once more. Stop being stupid, he thought. But those words fell victim to the blackness around him, consumed by the fog and his very own anxiety eating him from the inside. And so, his feet moved even quicker. And his heart beat harder. Adrenaline surged through him.

His thoughts spiralled. What if someone *did* get in? What if they're *already* in?

The wind created sinister noises behind him as it whipped through the fencing and slapped against the bars on the windows. It was like the scratching of a chalkboard; slowly, sinister – followed by a whisper. A child's whisper. Soft, yet loud enough to be heard. And as it grew, as he imagined the whispers as chatter, he felt someone behind him.

Breathing on his neck.

Watching.

Watching every single move.

Arms outstretched.

Waiting to pounce.

And then he realised *he was being watched*. There were hundreds of prisoners within the buildings surrounding him. And he pictured their eyes, the eyes of dangerous people, watching him as though he was prey. Like spectators in an auditorium, or hungry ghouls as he passed through limbo.

And he couldn't help but feel as though those eyes were free; that they followed him, joined by a hundred more with every step he took; every window he passed. And if their eyes were free, then so would their hands. And their mouths. Waiting to grab his ankles. Eager to taste his blood.

And he knew his thoughts were irrational. But he couldn't quell the fear. The wind, it amplified such with every gust. The laughs it created, the demonic laughter – as the prisoners conspired against him. And with every passing second, those conspiracies grew. He was an officer; they'd love to kill him. Torture him. And nobody would hear his screams, nobody would save him. The walls were too tall. He could scream right now and no one would hear.

He couldn't turn his head to dispel the fear, it had possessed him already, possessed every fibre of his panicked body. His head wouldn't move if he wanted it to. It was only focused on forwards. All he could move was his feet. Forwards. Forwards. Forwards!

For getting in...

FOR GETTING IN

FOR GETTING IN!

He really ought to sleep more he thought. These were just symptoms of his tiredness. But the atmosphere taunted him still. It brought an icy air with a ghostly chill that cut through him. It clothed his bald head like a set of dead hands caressing his skin.

ROAAAAAAAR!

The roar caused Bruce to freeze like a gargoyle. One leg suspended in the air, hands outstretched. Even the air in his lungs held tightly, fighting the urge to weep past his vocals and let out a scream.

And his heart stopped, leaving an unusual silence to animate the disturbing atmosphere around him. Because the laughter had stopped too, as if whatever had roared was enough to spook even the pits of Hell deep from within the prison.

Only seconds passed,

but it felt like hours.

Heart-wrenching hours.

Beads of sweat dripped from his forehead, from his nose, from most of his face, soaking into his black, prison-issued bomber jacket.

He wanted to leave his skin. To climb out of it. To leave this moment. To float away to a safe space. He'd never been so afraid in his entire life.

"Damien, you awake mate?" he heard a prisoner shout through his window from the closest building.

The familiarity of the noise brought him back to his senses. His heart beat once more. His breath released an exasperating sigh of relief. And suddenly he could hear lots of noises that his fear had blocked out. Shouts from other prisoners talking between blocks. A boat. Another boat.

A boat.

Yes, he thought. It must have been a boat, or a ship, sounding its horn. He'd heard it a thousand times before. The sea was on the other side of the wall; not directly, but close enough. A roar? There weren't even wolves in Scotland anymore. What was going to roar? The rabbits?

And just as he'd convinced himself, just as he'd made his move to continue forwards, a black shape darted across his peripheral vision.

It moved quickly.

Too quick for him to see what it was.

He screamed,

and broke into a run,

as fast as his heavy body could.

He fumbled one hand with his radio to call for Chris, and with his other, he tried to grab his baton. Neither worked though, and he clumsily tripped over his frightened feet, into a roll, and onto his back.

He squeezed his eyes shut and whimpered.

Make it quick, he thought, petrified.

Time froze once again, torturing him.

Maybe days passed. Because again, this moment, this moment felt like an eternity for Bruce.

But only seconds after falling, he heard purring.

Purring.

Rhythmic soft purring.

Like nectar to his ears, it was the sound of innocence rather than the imaginative monster he had let poison his mind.

He forced open his eyes to the 'prison cat' hovering over him.

The obsidian black molly boasted only one eye and was larger than most other cats Bruce knew. It had gotten fat killing rats within the prison, to which there was a plentiful supply. And yet as deadly a hunter as it was, it was a loving companion to the officers. And so, it purred away, rubbing its body against Bruce's.

Bruce heard a thunder of laughter in the distance. "Did anybody see that?"

"What?" shouted another prisoner.

Numerous lights turned on among nearby buildings.

"That fat baldy officer just shite-bagged it because of a cat."

"Is that what that scream was?"

More laughter.

Bruce ignored them and rubbed his hand against the cat's face.

"You gave me such a fright you little arse," said Bruce as he sat up.

He sighed a breath of relief, listening to the sound of his heart pounding throughout the night. It beat so strongly he could feel it pulsating through his head. He could also feel his shirt was soaked with sweat underneath his jacket. It stuck to him, his trousers too.

There was more laughter. But he didn't mind it in truth. Laughter. Actual laughter, not the callous taunting that he had pictured howling behind him moments ago. Innocent laughter, albeit at his expense, but harmless nonetheless.

"Is that him there?"

"Yeah mate, absolutely shit himself."

Bruce chuckled out loud. He expected a radio message of some sort, the control room officers would surely have seen him on the cameras. He could see the funny side of it. What a mess he'd gotten himself into. A grown-ass adult scared of the dark, scared of a bit of fog. He'd be hearing about this from his colleagues for weeks, probably months.

The night air suddenly felt so chill, so calming. Nothing scary about it. There never was. He'd done this for years, this same patrol, numerous times per night. Friday the thirteenth. Halloween. He'd done it all, and not once, not ever, had he been spooked like he was tonight.

"I'll tell you what kitty, I'll sure as hell sleep after this shift," he said petting the cat with his shaking fingers.

He stroked the cat for a few more minutes, enjoying the relaxing noise of her purring before he stood up.

"Best get back to it," he said, continuing forwards towards the end of his patrol.

Had he taken a moment to search the area to his left, however, in the darkest corner of the prison, between two buildings, where no light worked - he would have noticed the remains of the second jail cat.

The little that remained of him, that is.

Bones broken and twisted; crushed by a set of teeth that had easily crunched through, sat upon blood-stained grass. Not a flicker of flesh in sight...

CHAPTER 3
THE OLD CODGER

"Nightshift manager to Tango-Zulu-Five-Eight, message," crackled Chris over the radio.

"Send, Chris," replied Bruce.

"Meet me in Alpha Block, would you? Need to open a cell door."

"Received, over."

Bruce wondered what the issue was as he walked towards Alpha Block. It was likely the usual; two fighters needing separated because one wanted to sleep and the other wanted to watch TV.

He walked over with a grump in his step. He just wanted coffee already. Was that too much to ask? He had a long night ahead of him and his little episode had usurped the meagre energy he had woken with this morning. He needed refuelling. No, *he needed fuelling in general*. And yet, they needed him, so he would have to wait a moment longer. Why? The officers inside each block weren't allowed to open cell doors at night without him and the manager present. Skeleton staff and all that.

He arrived before Chris.

"Control Room message, over."

"Send."

"Can you please take the electronic lock off Alpha please, over?" he shouted through his radio as he placed a manual key into the lock at the same time.

"Alpha you said Bruce? Sorry, I can't see you, some of the cameras are down."

"Yes, Alpha please, over," he replied as he watched the CCTV camera moving frantically above him.

"Control Room received and completed, over."

Bruce turned the handle counterclockwise and pushed open the heavy metal door which was at least four inches thick.

After double-checking to make sure he had locked the door properly, he approached the front desk to greet the two officers in charge of patrolling the block.

The first was Lydia, an older lady in her fifties. Her blonde hair was tied into a bun which showcased her sharp, pretty features. The second was Greg, an annoying eighteen-year-old scrotum whose work ethic was as productive as a steak pie in a vegan eatery. He was short, with buzz-cut brown hair and glasses that sat upon his pointy nose.

Bruce looked up and down the block gauging the atmosphere. It was unusually loud tonight, with so much noise it conversely muffled itself. Bruce struggled to pick out any particular conversation from the screaming prisoners.

There were four landings, or galleries, and a set of stairs in the centre of the block which led up to each of the four levels. There was open space in between, and Bruce could see right up to the glass ceiling forty feet above. Cells ran down both the left and right side, on each level, including the ground floor.

It was an old style of prison, Victorian, evident by the matured décor. Like a sad rain cloud about to brew into a vicious storm, the entire block looked as dark and grimy as it was lonely. Off-white paint peeled from stairs, as it did railings, revealing a boring grey metal underneath; or a dirty ember from where rust had set in. The walls were freshly painted in all fairness but again, dull grey. As if the intention was to suck any life and all happiness from both staff and prisoners. Even the net between the first floor, attached to the bottom of the railings and covering the empty space, was torn from where people had thrown things over. Or worse – jumped, adding melancholy to the depressing atmosphere.

"So what's up?" asked Bruce, giving his attention to Lydia.

"Leo Malone," sighed Lydia.

"Ugh," moaned Bruce. "That old codger is the reason I can't have a coffee?"

"He's having an episode," shrugged Lydia, sipping at her own hot brew.

"He always has them," replied Bruce. He stared at the cup as a fox would a rabbit. "Mind if I have a sip?"

She laughed. "You think I'm letting your chin scruff anywhere near my cup? It's dripping. You're soaked. Did you run here?"

"Long story," replied Bruce awkwardly. "Go on, let me have a sip, I'm like a walking zombie."

Lydia shook her head and continued her story. "Anyway, this episode is different. It's not his usual breakdown. Claims he saw a monster outside of his window. Spawn of the Devil, he says, if you can believe that."

"Probably the jail cat," muttered Bruce, hiding his own embarrassment.

"Well, whatever it is. He's thrashed his head against the wall, broken his knuckles too. Smashed up his television and his radio. There are sharps everywhere. We will need to move him to a safer cell and give him first aid."

"First aid?" scoffed Bruce. "He should be in a mental hospital, not here."

"Agreed," replied Lydia. "But that's above our pay grade. You can have some of my coffee by the way, I've got a whole tub of instant in the back, but the kettle will need boiled again."

Bruce grabbed her head playfully and kissed her forehead almost causing her to spill her cup. "You know how much I love you, don't you?"

"Too much," she said with a smile, as she wiped away his saliva.

Bruce didn't hesitate. He almost sprinted into the small staff room, suddenly finding motivation.

The room was no larger than an average appliance room with just enough space for a sink, worktop, mini fridge, overflowing bin and battered old couch. He grabbed a mug from the only cupboard underneath the sink and filled it with a mountain-sized spoonful.

"So what have you been up to so far?" he shouted from the office as he noticed the TV on the wall was oddly switched off. "Nothing decent on the telly? I presume you'll be watching YouTube all night? BBC iPlayer?"

"Internet's off," grunted Greg.

"Off?" asked Bruce as he watched the kettle boil, praying for it to quicken.

Lydia nodded. "And all the TV channels. Only DVDs are working."

"That's strange," said Bruce. He thought about the news article he wanted to google. It was silly but something bugged him. He wasn't sure why, but something inside him suspected there might be a link between the article and the behaviours of the managers. "Like completely off?"

"No connection whatsoever," moaned Greg. "Pain in the arse because the football is on tonight."

"Ah," noted Bruce as he looked at the bleeping intercom next to the staff desk. "Explains all the noise in here. Unhappy customers."

"Been buzzing constantly. At least the banging of the doors has ceased for now."

"There I thought Greg was just doing the bare minimum again and not answering the intercom," laughed Bruce.

Greg grunted but didn't bite.

"We ready to rock and roll?" asked Chris as he appeared out of nowhere. Nobody had heard the outside door open, or close. But then, the heavy metal choir of prisoners animating the block could have drowned out a hurricane.

"Ugh. Just as the kettle boiled," sighed Bruce. He clutched his chest imitating pain in his heart. "You know I'll be way more productive once I've had a coffee if we just sit for five?"

Chris shook his head. "Let's go. Coffee can wait, this can't."

With haste, they opened the cell door; another thick impenetrable steel chunk. And like everything else, the paint peeled from it revealing its rusted and yet ever so robust bone underneath.

The door brushed against a mountain of mess that Leo had created on the floor. Cups, plates, paperwork, and DVDs. Anything and everything he owned was sitting in a chaotic mess. His CD Player was smashed to pieces. His TV too. And right enough there was blood across the walls. It dribbled down his hands, and forehead, onto his naked, skinny body. He was so malnourished that his ribs were as visible as the veins underneath his skin.

The mess made the cell seem even smaller than it already was. Immediately to Bruce's right was a brown-stained plastic toilet. This sat next to a small sink protruding from the wall - so miniscule that it was more suited as a bird bath. A wire bed frame with a mattress thinner than a slab of chocolate sat along the left wall. And in the far right corner of the tiny box cell was a small shelf area where most other prisoners placed their televisions.

"Sit on the bed for me," commanded Chris.

"Y-you n-need to g-get me out of h-here," begged Leo frantically. He fell to his knees, clasping his hands. He did not care for the cockroach that scurried from paper underneath his knee. Neither did anyone actually. It was a common sight.

"Bed," pointed Chris. "And tell me what's going on."

"M-monster, o-outside," shivered Leo as he picked up his shaking body and sat on the creaky bed. "T-T-Teeth l-like knives. F-Fingers l-like s-swords. F-F-a-ast. Very f-f-fast."

"You know there's no monsters here," assured Lydia. "It's safe here."

Leo jumped up and frantically pointed towards the window on the back wall. "L-lie lies! I saw it! I saw."

"Sit down," demanded Chris. "We're going to move you to a different cell, okay? You'll be safe there tonight."

Leo shook his head. "No, no. Y-You d-don't u-understand. M-Monster outside. It'll get me in any cell. It will get us all! I need out of the p-prison. We a-all n-need to go. Nowhere safe. We go n-now!"

"Look, Leo," stated Bruce. "I'm going to look outside, make sure it's safe and then we will go to your new cell, okay? We're friends, aren't we? You'll believe me when I tell you it's all good?"

Leo nodded.

And so, Bruce dragged his boots through the mess on the floor and looked out the window, past the metal bars thick enough for only two fingers to squeeze through and the clouded plastic beyond that. He expected to see the prison cat once more.

But he didn't...

A minute passed.

And Bruce hadn't moved.

Frozen in

TERROR.

Like Medusa herself had looked into his soul.

Suddenly, Bruce screamed, *roared*, in outright fright at the gentle touch on his shoulder. He was so spooked, so scared, that he pushed Chris to the floor, not realising it was him who'd touched him.

"What the fuck Bruce?" spat Chris as he quickly picked himself up.

"S-sorry," squealed Bruce. His once-tanned face was paler than the white of the moon. "S-sorry."

"I k-knew it!" screamed Leo as he tried to run out of the cell, only stopped by Lydia pushing him back. "Help! H-help! The m-monsters are going to kill us."

"I saw it," muttered Bruce, whimpering almost. "I saw it."

And he did.

This wasn't his overimaginative imagination again. This wasn't a cat, or any such harmless creature.

No.

No.

No.

This was two sets of green daggered eyes that had stared into his with a dangerous hunger. This was the eyes of two large monsters. Their silhouettes had burned themselves into Bruce's mind. The claws. The teeth. It was just as the old codger had described. He couldn't tell what the creatures were but they were not of this world. They were spawns of the devil no doubt.

Bruce pushed past his colleagues and out of the cell.

"Lock that door," he heard Chris angrily shout to Lydia as both them and Greg followed.

There was immediate banging. "L-let m-me out. D-don't leave m-me to d-die."

"I'll get back to you in five Leo, all right," assured Lydia as the door clicked into locked position.

"You," roared Chris, pointing a finger in Bruce's face. "What the fuck was that? What do you think you're playing at?"

Bruce looked like an empty shell. *"S-something got in."*

CHAPTER 4
DATE WITH A DINOSAUR

It took around ten minutes for Bruce to recover, to compose himself. He'd locked himself in the staff bathroom watching the colour return to his face in the cracked mirror. He debated staying there all night. But the thought, just knowing what was outside, like he was a mouse in a trap, caused a permanent shiver to consume him.

And so, he knew what he had to do - he had to leave the prison. The monsters were between the fencing and the wall - 'no man's land.' That's where he'd seen them. He'd be fine if he moved now. The Control Room would radio if an alarm was triggered - if a fence was touched - so he'd know when and where the creatures dared climb. Or that's what he told himself. Just enough to get his legs going.

He burst through the bathroom door pushing past his colleagues with little regard. Both Chris and Lydia had been banging at the door the entire time trying to usher him out.

"Bruce, where are you going?" asked Chris furiously as he followed him out of the building.

"Home," replied Bruce as the night air hit him. It soaked into him, tickling him, teasing him with another episode of terror. It seemed so dark again. But he had to move, and so he did, before his fear devoured him once more.

Or something worse.

"You can't just go home," shouted Chris as he manually locked the door and radioed the control room to reapply the electronic lock now that they'd left. He caught up with Bruce. "You're on duty. Please, let's go inside."

"I *am* going home. So open the front door at the vestibule for me please."

"Bruce, be reasonable here," insisted Chris as he matched Bruce's quick feet. "You'll get investigated for this. You'll get dismissed. This is gross misconduct. Come on, let's go inside already. It's cold out here."

"I'll do it myself if you won't. I know where the keys are kept. Or I'll smash the glass. You can add that to your investigation!"

"Bruce! Inside now!"

"Will you stop telling me to go inside," shouted Bruce as he stopped and faced Chris. "What's your deal?"

Chris looked uneasy as he looked around, like an insect in a spider's den.

"What are you looking for, huh? The thing I saw? Cause I fucking saw it Chris," pleaded Bruce. "I fucking saw it. A fucking monster. Two of them. I don't know what they were, but the faster I'm out of here the better."

"You're just tired. Go have a lie down and we'll talk about this in an hour or two when you've got a fresh head on you."

"Tired?" tutted Bruce. The anger gave him strength, overpowering his worry. In those seconds he didn't care, or even think, about the bait he was presenting himself by standing still. "Did I hallucinate the headquarters managers too?"

"They were just -"

"They were just what, eh?" he screamed, interrupting him. "They were spooked. You're fucking spooked, you're being weird. And why's the internet off? The TV's too? Coincidence? What do they not want us to know? What's this experiment that went wrong? What's the newspaper on about?"

"Newspaper?" replied Chris, confused. "It's just, it's nothing, Bruce, okay? Trust me. You probably just saw a rat."

"A rat? A fucking rat with meat cleavers for fingers? Stop lying! Just tell me, tell me what the fuck is going on! What the hell were those things? Tell me what you know!"

"I've told you already."

Bruce waved at him, flicking him off, and continued to walk towards the front of the prison in a stomping march.

"Look, I don't know much -" shouted Chris as he tried to catch up. "But what I can tell you -"

ROAAAAAAAAAR!

The ice-chilling war cry caused both to halt their movements.

"You heard that?" Bruce whispered, almost too afraid to utter a word.

Chris nodded uneasily.

"Sure it wasn't a rat?" spat Bruce as he pulled his baton from his pocket and drew it. It would normally command obedience when drawn and yet it sat on Bruce's left shoulder like a deflated balloon, dampened by the ominous atmosphere that gnawed it whole.

ROAAAAAAAAAR!

The second roar was louder, closer, like a thunder bearing the cruellest lightning. Lightning that would destroy a city in its entirety.

TOO CLOSE! The snarls were like whispers in their ears, climbing into their skins and licking at their bones.

Both broke into a sprint

"Wait!" panted Chris. "I put a manual lock on the security entrance door, your fingerprint won't work, you won't get through it."

"Then where's the keys for that?" screamed Bruce, as Chris, fitter than he, ran in front. "You've hidden them, haven't you? We're not supposed to get out, are we?"

But Chris ignored him.

The night shift manager pulled his radio from his belt, changed the frequency and frantically started to speak.

"This is HMP Kirkwood, monster on site, I repeat, initiate..."

Bruce didn't know what he heard first.

The screeching from the materialised monster in front of them or the squealing from Chris' skull popping in one powerful crunch. Even then, was it the crunch of bone shattering that Bruce heard, or the squelch as Chris' brains were turned into organic mush?

Bruce was frozen in anguish. Not a blink, not a breath, not a heartbeat. Not even a thought dared flicker across his mind as if a lack of animation would somehow make him invisible.

The creature stood staring with a purring curiosity.

It was around five feet tall with a long, narrow snout bearing shark-like teeth. Teeth that continued to grind the remains of the man Bruce once called friend. Red, scaly skin decorated its entire body and camouflaged any and all blood splatter. To which there would have been plenty, given the red mist cloaking the beast whole – the fog soaked up Chris' blood like a hungry hyena. It stood on hinged ankles, with talons mirroring a reaper's sickle which were just as pointed as the claws protruding from its slender arms.

'Was it a dinosaur?' questioned a thought creeping into Bruce's mind. Something else? A demon?

Its green eyes surveyed Bruce up and down with little interest, like he was but a fly. It looked towards the baton between his fingers for a few extra seconds as if analysing, deciding whether it was a threat, or a mere inconvenience. Presuming the latter, the creature ignored Bruce and took to mauling the warm corpse of Chris instead. It ripped into his body as easily as tearing bread, allowing guts and blood to spray into the air like a woodchipper spitting out remains.

Bruce eventually breathed, not by choice, but by necessity, for he hadn't taken a breath in the two minutes he had frightfully stared at the creature.

And then his legs moved.

Fight or flight.

And he chose flight. His legs were already moving before his brain had decided, but he wasn't going to argue. What would the measly stick between his fingers do against a creature like that?

He dared not run directly ahead though, he dared not test the creature's mercy. If such even existed. He expected the creature to chase as soon as his legs had moved. Every second, every millisecond was an expectation to be its next course.

He ran to his left, to the closest cell block; Charlie.

It was particularly quiet. Not a shout, not a scream. Just an eerie silence clothed the entire building. Like a candle burned out, the building felt abandoned.

As he approached the front door, he grabbed his radio to message Control to remove the electronic lock, but the connection was gone. The small digital screen was disconnected from every channel. He didn't know why. Was it the same reason the phones were down? All he knew was he couldn't radio to get in. Worse: he couldn't radio for help. But he didn't have time to dwell on it, not now. He needed shelter.

And so, he ran around the side, towards the back, towards an emergency entry – a contingency if the electronics ever failed. It required two manual keys. Both in his possession. Carrying each set of keys on his person defeated the point of the security mechanism but Chris allowed it for convenience. And thank fuck, thought Bruce.

He fumbled with both sets of keys, dropping them. They bounced off the concrete and back into his hands as he pulled on the lanyard which both were attached to - itself attached to his belt.

He tried the lock again. But his shaky fingers dropped the keys once more. And even when his vibrating hands managed to find the composure to hold the key and place it into the first lock, it didn't turn. It was the incorrect key. There were at least six or seven keys in each bunch, but with his mind possessed by panic and dread, he couldn't find the correct one. He'd suddenly forgotten every trick, every pattern.

And the more he tried, the more he stressed. His fingers became sweatier. His thoughts could only focus on teeth sinking into his flesh. And when they didn't, they focused on

Chris' exploding skull. So much until his fear had replaced the image with his own face. Until his memory had given the creature a cruel, grinning smile. A smile that grew and grew until it had wrapped itself around his neck whole.

By his eighth attempt, he'd unlocked the first lock and by a miracle unlocked the next on the first try.

When he finally entered, and locked the door behind him... He screamed a piercing scream so loud, so intense that it championed the roar of the red monster...

CHAPTER 5
THE HORROR HALLWAY

R^{ed.} Red.

Red.

RED!

All Bruce could see was red. Despite the dull look of the Victorian prison, it had been animated by the deep vibrant crimson of blood. Brought to life by the death around it.

He retched. And retched. And retched. And retched. The sick erupted everywhere. Over his trousers, over the floor... over a corpse lying next to him.

A CORPSE!

And not the only one. All around him. Bodies. As lifeless as the prison itself.

He looked up and down the block. Prisoners. Mauled. Blood dripped down from the floors above, spilling through the gaps in the railings, creating a waterfall of tortured red.

He didn't want to stare anymore, he wanted to close his eyes, and yet he couldn't. In utter disbelief, his vision looked up and down the entire hallway of the block, absorbing every pitiful flavour of the horrific image.

Chunks of unrecognisable flesh sat in mishappen piles. Once arms, legs, bodies... *once people*... the mess was nothing more than organic chaos. Splintered bones protruded from mountains of meat, others sat nearby licked clean of flesh. It was a battlefield, a slaughterhouse.

Clothes. The blue shades of both torn jeans and jumpers clung to beaten flesh, the only indicator identifying the mess as once living humans, and not that of diced animals.

Bruce vomited again.

He wanted to turn and leave.

But where would he go? Face to face with the monster outside?

And yet here, in among this deathly disaster, was it much better? What if one of those creatures were inside? One of those ... dare he think it... dinosaurs inside? No human could create such a graveyard. It had to be one of the creatures. The question is, was it still here? And if it was, if it was still lurking in the shadows... what if there were others? Worse... deadlier?

His mind fell into despair. He felt stuck, trapped by the devil with demons on every path. Monsters outside, monsters inside.

He needed a phone. His radio was still disconnected. He hated himself for thinking it. But there, at the other end of the hallway, on the staff desk, sat the desk phone. He needed the police. The army. Any fucking person. Because he wasn't it. He *needed* that phone.

He moved slowly, baton drawn, holding his breath so the stench of fresh decay didn't cause him to empty the last remnants of his stomach.

His boots stuck to the sticky blood and pulled with every step like cheese being plucked apart from a pizza. It squelched, masking the squeak that would normally be heard from his boots. The thought of standing on blood, on the remains of a person... no, he couldn't think about it. He mustn't. He had to move on, he had to keep moving forwards. And so, he forced his brain to shut down. To ignore the corpses around him. To think only of the phone, only of his own survival.

His feet crunched over glass, to his surprise. It caused him to freeze, one foot suspended in the air. The noise echoed throughout the entire block and for a few tense seconds, his heartbeat along with.

He looked up, towards the ceiling, towards the sunroof covering a third of it, as he lowered his foot cautiously. Only now did he realise the wind rushing through. It had been smashed completely as if something heavy had fallen through. Could the creature really have climbed onto the roof? Is that how it got in? A building this tall? And if it could, if it did... then the walls wouldn't stop them.

Bruce carefully bypassed the glass, as he tried to reduce the noise from his steps as much as possible. As he crept along, nearing the staff desk, he noticed not all cell doors were open, only around half. Maybe even slightly less. And yet silence clung to the air. Not a whisper from a single person still alive. He could only imagine those who were, were as frightened as he, daring not utter a sound.

Suddenly he was attacked by an unexpected force causing him to drop his baton. Whatever charged at him, had the strength to take him several meters until he was thrown into a closed cell door.

As he dropped, his face landed next to the decapitated head of a prisoner. The man's sunken eyes were pried open, his mouth still ajar; as if he screamed to the very last second he breathed, as if he was still screaming beyond his life, into the afterlife.

And like a virus, the silent scream spread into Bruce's lungs and he too screamed. The scream was quickly cut short though as a heavy fist beat into his side, stealing the air from his lungs. And then another, and another. Punch after punch causing him to brace.

He tried to push the unknown assailant away with scrambled hands but felt a powerful kick to his face as a consequence.

"Stop," he heard someone whisper as he tried to blindly crawl away, fingers clawing at puddled blood. "We need him."

"Yeah we need him to know who's boss," he heard, as another foot smashed into his face. "Isn't that right, fat boy?"

His head hit off the concrete wall with so much force, he was but a thread away from falling unconscious.

"Stop," muttered Bruce, dazed, as he sat himself up against the wall. He could feel blood dribble from both his nose and lip. "You've made your point, whatever that was."

"How about you give me your keys and then we will talk?"

Bruce looked up as he caught his breath. Four prisoners surrounded him, hunched over like hungry vultures. He guessed the six-foot steroid junkie was the one who had been attacking him. He seemed to be in charge. Less shaken up than the other three. He looked tough in general though. Strong; thick neck, bulging biceps and a jaw sharp enough to rival the creature's claws.

"My keys don't work in here, fool," hissed Bruce.

"Fool?"

Bruce felt another kick to the face. The skin on his forehead split, instantly causing a volcano of blood to explode.

"Want to try that again, smart arse?"

"I'm the outside patrol," panted Bruce in pain. "I don't have cell door keys. Where even are the officers who should be here?"

"Do I look like I need cell keys?" taunted the prisoner as he waved a pair in front of his face. "Your colleague was nice and opened a door once that dinosaur walked over the roof. Managed to free quite a few of us before the thing -"

Bruce looked towards where the man was pointing. Just above them, Bruce could see an arm hanging over the barrier; white shirt now mostly red. A pang ran through him, squeezing at his heart, but he did not wish to know the identity. Not now. He would mourn later. If he survived that long.

"We need your keys to get out of the building," said a softer voice, more politely. The man looked timid in general with scrawny features and nerdy glasses. "Please, and then we'll leave you alone."

"Look -" said Bruce.

The larger prisoner stepped on Bruce's fingers causing him to cry out.

"I could pry the keys off your dead body or you give me them now and I'll let you live?"

"There's electronic locks on the door," groaned Bruce in agony, as he swiftly unclipped both sets of keys from his belt with his other hand. "It won't make a difference. The door I came in with is a failsafe, opened from the outside only," lied Bruce.

"They're off, the electronic locks," said the prisoner as he stepped off of Bruce's fingers. "Like your radios, the phones. Everything's off."

"Off?" muttered Bruce. "Phones too?"

The prisoner nodded. "All the cameras too."

Bruce looked up towards the wall near the staff door and true enough, the red blinking light which normally flashed when recording was absent.

"Should we get back to opening the rest of the cells, Pascal?" suggested one of the prisoners.

The large prisoner, Pascal, shook his head. "No time, in case another one of those dinosaurs comes. Got to look after ourselves."

Dinosaurs. That's the second time they'd used that word. Which meant they thought as much as he did. The deadly demon he'd faced, they deadly demon they'd faced, was none other than an ancient creature from the past.

"Where's the one that was here?" Bruce dared ask.

Pascal chuckled and pointed to a mutilated mess next to a pool table about fifty yards away. It was smaller than the one Bruce had encountered but boasted the same features. Scaly skin, vicious weaponry; a walking crocodile. A real-life, albeit dead, dinosaur...

As Bruce stared in disbelief, he could see multiple weapons protruding from its body; broken mops and pool cues, makeshift blades, anything sharp enough to pierce its leather skin.

"So, they *can* be killed..." muttered Bruce.

"Not without a fight," replied Pascal as he turned towards the direction of the door. There were numerous large gashes across his back which spilt blood down to his legs. They were so deep that Bruce could see the scarlet muscle underneath. He could see the very fibres of the muscles move as the man walked.

After considerable trial and error with the keys and a punch towards the wall, Pascal unlocked the door before each of the prisoners exited with haste.

Bruce sat against the wall, catching his breath, taking a second to process the ill imagery around him. The bloodbath around him... it certainly must have been one hell of a fight. Fifty bodies? Sixty? He couldn't tell how many were around him; how many were slaughtered upstairs. All he knew was he was but one man. What chance did he have?

"What do I do now?" moaned Bruce in despair. He looked up to the ceiling with a quivering lip, and a twitching face, as anger welled up inside him. "Is there a God? Is this a test? Well, I fucking hate it. I concede. You hear me in your pearly white fucking chair? Your fancy silk robes? Was this your doing, huh? Some part of your bright fucking plan? Look at this fucking mess? Look at it! How is this divine? How is -"

"Bruce is that you?" whispered a timid voice interrupting him.

Bruce recognised the voice instantly, causing him to gasp. But he didn't believe it. Not at first.

"Bruce?" said the voice, louder this time.

"Myla? Myla, is that really you?"

A woman climbed out of a fire hatch right next to him, a small red square built into the wall which housed fire extinguishers. It was a perfect spot for a petite lady such as herself to hide.

She stood tall and brushed dust from her uniform. She was brunette, with amber-coloured eyes and soft features which were made harsher by the tattoos across her neck and on both arms. It was the little mole above her lip that Bruce loved so much though, that was his favourite feature of hers.

"Myla?" said Bruce again.

She immediately took him into an embrace.

He squeezed her in close. He couldn't believe it. Her. Here. Now. She shouldn't be. And tonight, of all nights? The thought crippled his heart.

"I didn't know you were working tonight," he managed to say. He didn't know what else to say. Married for sixteen years. Parted for four months. Hadn't spoken for the last three. So much to say and yet so little at the same time.

She sniffled. "We're in a goddam nightmare and that's what you've got to say to me?"

"Overtime, is it?" said Bruce, trying to humour her. "Finally paying to fix that nose of yours?"

"I hate you," she sniffled, pulling him tighter.

And he squeezed some more, holding back his own tears.

"What's going on Bruce, is this real?" she asked as she pulled apart from their embrace after around a minute. She painfully analysed the massacre around her, fixating on the monster's corpse. "Dinosaurs? Please tell me it's not real. It can't be real. It can't..."

He stared into her eyes, thinking them as beautiful as the day he'd first met her. All the problems they'd ever had suddenly seemed so petty; every argument meaningless. "It just got real," he sighed.

She grabbed his hand and stroked it gently, looking him up and down.

"Ugh your trousers are covered in your own sick, and there are chunks in your beard!" she said with disgust as she recoiled and pulled away. "Ugh, and I hugged you."

"Like that time in Vegas, remember? You know, after we had all those peach shots?"

They both chuckled.

And it felt like the last few months hadn't existed, it felt normal. He didn't know what was going on, or how this situation came to be. But that didn't matter. He only knew he had to stay strong, despite the fear that washed over him. Despite every cell in his body wanting to cry and collapse into nothingness. He had to protect her. At all costs.

Just how he would do so was the impossible question.

CHAPTER 6
THE RADIO

"So, what's the plan?" asked Myla as she picked up her jacket from the desk, ensuring no blood splatter had reached the fibres. "Head straight for the lobby?"

Bruce shook his head. "Chris said the keys were moved. And anyway, the security doors have a manual override on them, we'd need those keys too wherever they are."

"What? You're kidding?"

"I know, I know. It must be why I patrolled myself, whilst he hid them."

"Hid them? Why? Where?" she replied, puzzled. "Well, we need to go find them."

"In a jail this size?" replied Bruce, shaking his head. "They could be anywhere."

"Well let's find *him*, make him tell us."

Bruce looked away, awkwardly. There was a sadness in his gaze, he hadn't had a second to process, to grieve yet. Chris was more than his manager; he was a friend. A good one at that.

"Oh... no..." said Myla softly as she noticed the pain in Bruce's eyes. "Is he- is he?"

"Dead," sighed Bruce, nodding. "Slaughtered. He didn't get to tell me where the keys were either before you ask."

There was a moment's silence as neither knew what to say. As neither knew how they were to escape the nightmare they'd found themselves victim to.

"I still don't get why he would move the keys?" moaned Myla. "If he knew what was going on, he'd want out just as much as us?"

"Perhaps he didn't know the extent," suggested Bruce. His expression turned dark. "Perhaps they don't want us to get out, and perhaps he was part of it. I'd put money on it, them wanting us to stay inside, in the dark. It would explain why the phones are down. And everything else. We're cut off from the outside world and that's not a coincidence."

"But why? Did they know this was going to happen? That these..." she shook her head in disbelief. "Dinosaurs Bruce. Real-life dinosaurs. I can't get my head around it. How many even are there? And why here? A prison in the middle of nowhere?"

Bruce shrugged his shoulders. "I wish I had the answers, but I don't. Maybe, maybe they had some sort of plan. Before Chris was.... -" There was a pause. "... Killed. He was changing the frequency..."

Bruce's eyes lit up.

"What is it, Bruce?"

"That's it! Our way out! The radio! Maybe Chris' radio will work. I think he was contacting somebody outside, outside of the walls. Our internal frequencies might be down but maybe an external channel will work. And he seemed to have access to that frequency. He was speaking to it."

"That's great!" grinned Myla. "No, that's brilliant! Let's go get it then!"

Bruce looked up with an awkward sigh.

"He died holding it, didn't he?" asked Myla as despair ate into her words.

Bruce nodded and pointed. "Right outside that door." He watched the door slap against the frame every two seconds as the wind caught it. *It was unlocked* – a small silver lining among an ugly thread of misery.

"Looks like they left it open for us."

Bruce nodded thankfully.

"But do you think the creature is still there?" asked Myla sheepishly, as her lips cowered away from speaking the words, imagining the worst.

"Even if it wasn't, we'd be out in the open."

"Do we have another choice?"

Bruce knew they didn't. They could get the radio, and maybe get help. Probably get killed. Or they could stay here, as bait, and... also probably get killed. Neither were favourable options but at least one had a positive outlook, a chance at survival as slim as it was.

"Don't go without us!" came a scream alongside the kick of a door.

Another prisoner joined in, banging at his door too. "At least open the doors! Please!"

Both Bruce and Myla stared at each other. They both had the same look in their eyes. Both torn. Both torn between empathy and their duties.

"I've got children on the outside!"

"Me too, she's only six!"

Others joined in, pleading, begging, saying everything and anything to be let free.

"We can't," said Bruce guiltily. He'd whispered, as if ashamed of the decision he'd made.

"What if we opened one door and left them with cell keys?" suggested Myla. "We won't need my keys out there, they're useless. And the other prisoners did leave that door open for us, they could have locked us in."

Bruce shook his head. "Do you trust them? Trust them not to strike at us? To take our batons? They're safer behind a locked door, look around us. Having them run loose to end up like this?"

"I know but it doesn't feel right."

"We get help, and then the help can save them. We don't need them getting in our way."

Bruce could see by Myla's expression that she didn't like it, but she didn't disagree either. Because as much as her eyes filled with pain and guilt, her head nodded in understanding.

Bruce stroked her face. "I need to keep you safe, and I will, okay?"

He picked up his baton from the floor. It was covered in congealed blood causing him to shiver as his fingers wrapped around the sticky metal. Despite such, he placed it on his shoulder, ready to strike, and crept towards the door.

Bruce pushed it open warily, letting the cold air slice through him.

"Argh!"

He jumped in fright causing Myla to scream behind him.

"What?" she squealed, panicked – eyes almost bursting from her skull. "What, what is it?"

Bruce chuckled, embarrassed. "The wind blew some rubbish, I got a scare."

"Fucking hell Bruce," moaned Myla. She scrambled past his arm and pushed the door open herself.

"Myla!"

But she wasn't kidding around.

She peered her dark-haired head outside, looking each way before storming forward towards the corpse around fifty or sixty meters away.

"Wait," commanded Bruce as he grabbed her shoulder and pulled her back. From the wall to the left of the door, he tore off a first aid box and threw it with all his strength towards Chris' body.

"Wait," said Bruce again, still holding onto Myla's shoulder.

A minute passed and nothing.

No movement.

No sign of any creature.

Only the eerie wind teasing the hairs across their entire body.

And so, they moved forwards.

Bruce took lead as he approached his friend's corpse. He dreaded what he would see. Every step forwards was as reluctant as the last. But he knew he had to.

As expected, his stomach churned when he arrived. He turned his head away instantly and forcibly brought it back around, prying his eyes open to absorb the ghastly sight.

The head was unrecognisable, the little left of it. There were a few chunks of pink and grey sitting in pools of red, covered in shards of white dust; the remains of skull. The body was much the same; most had been eaten. Clothes too, like a chocolate too Godly to unwrap - Chris had been eaten whole.

Bruce felt the urge to vomit again, as he knew what he had to do next. Because he couldn't see the radio among the deathly leftovers.

Still holding on to his baton with his left, he dug his right hand deep into Chris' remaining flesh. It was already cold. Mushy-feeling. Like running his hand across uncooked chicken fillets or fresh mince.

He gagged, and gagged, and gagged, and gagged.

He tried to distract himself as he fumbled among his friend's innards. He tried not to think about it, tried not to think about how his fingers wrapped around what was formerly intestines. Or how they pioneered through shredded liver and kidney.

"It's here!" shouted Bruce, quickly retreating his hand from Chris' remains.

The radio itself was soaked in blood. Strips of flesh embedded itself between buttons. But still, the display lit up showing a signal somewhere. It had worked! Their plan worked!

He turned towards Myla with a beaming smile.

It just as quickly faded.

Horror struck his heart.

"Don't move," he mouthed.

But she couldn't.

And she wouldn't.

She was as motionless as the buildings around her. She was petrified, gripped by terror.

This dinosaur was different, the one standing only a couple of meters in front of her, fixated on Bruce. It was larger, probably by a foot, maybe even two. Feathers; green, blue and yellow covered its back. They stood upright like a peacock's tail making it appear even larger. And its teeth and claws? Just as harsh and pointy as they'd expect. *Just as deadly*

And then it charged.

Towards Bruce.

He didn't have time to turn or run. The creature was quick, as quick as he could blink. It pushed off its powerful hind legs throwing itself through the air like an Olympian.

As the creature closed in, Bruce swung his baton. It whizzed through the air as powerfully as Bruce could swing, connecting with the left side of the dinosaur's brass skull.

Crack!

Like a gambling man, Bruce squeezed his eyes closed as the baton struck. In that second, he hoped, he prayed that the noise was the dinosaur's skull erupting to pieces. A tiny part of him even dared imagine victory – dared picture the creature's head splitting like the Red Sea.

As he opened them... he realised how wrong he was.

His baton had made the noise.

It had split into multiple pieces leaving a pointless handle between his fingers which he soon dropped.

There was a large fissure upon the monster's lizard face from where its leather skin burst. Yellow blood spilt, blinding one of its eyes.

And yet it didn't seem phased.

It didn't even hesitate.

It lunged forwards once more.

Bruce's left hand instinctively clenched, his arm rose, and he threw a punch with every bit of strength he could muster.

Right

into

the

dinosaur's

mouth.

"AHHHHHHHHHHHHHHHHHHHHHHHH!"

Even through his own screams, Bruce could hear the squelch and crunch as his forearm was torn clean off at the elbow. The powerful jaw only needed one bite to break through bone, ligament and tendon.

And then his legs ran, and he along with.

"Bruce!" shouted Myla.

But he couldn't hear her. His body was on autopilot, full sprint, throwing blood in all directions as his stump moved back and forth trying to propel his body further. His other hand, without even thinking about it, held onto the radio. He didn't even know where he was going, he had no plan. Just survive. Just run!

Just run, run, run!

Run!

RUN!

RUN!

The crimson monster who'd killed Chris appeared out of thin air as it had before, already in full charge towards Bruce.

And as he squeezed his eyes shut, waiting for his imminent death, he felt the whoosh of the creature rush past him. *Past him.*

"MYLA!" screamed his brain as his senses started to return. He couldn't leave Myla. And now there were two!

He turned, no longer caring about himself, finding control of his own body once more.

He had to save Myla.

But as he stared, as he ran back towards her, she wasn't in danger. Not immediately anyway.

The dinosaurs, like rivals, charged into each other. Like two bulls or lions, they butted heads with all of their might. As if a battle for territory, as if this new raptor-like dinosaur, the feathered one, had tasted the spoils of the red dinosaur. As if Bruce's arm had been claimed already.

Bruce failed to peel his eyes away as he watched the dinosaurs claw and bite at each other. As they snarled. As they roared. It was a sight to champion an Ancient Rome gladiator battle.

He didn't realise himself getting weaker either, he was so fixated.

As fixated as the creatures were with each other. Because neither noticed Myla run past them.

She grabbed Bruce by his jacket and pulled him away from the battle, just as his eyes closed and his world turned black...

CHAPTER 7
GREG AND LYDIA

"Do you think they're coming back?" asked Greg. He was currently eating his third packet of crisps, after having chomped through two whole chocolate bars and a yogurt.

"It's weird," admitted Lydia as they continued to listen to the roars of Leroy echo throughout the block. His unrest was causing other prisoners to shout and kick at their doors. First the lack of football and now this. She was getting a headache.

"Doesn't signal a good start to the week, does it?" sighed Greg between bites, letting crumbs fall onto the dusty dirt-stained floor.

"I'm going to radio him," replied Lydia.

And yet, as Lydia clicked the button on her radio to connect, nothing happened. She looked at her screen: no signal.

"What's up?" asked Greg as he watched Lydia turn her radio on and off.

"Check your radio for me, are you connected?"

"Huh, strange," replied Greg. "I'm not actually."

Lydia grabbed the desk phone. "I'll check with others in the other blocks."

Yet as she dialled the first number, there was no input.

"This is off too," she said, confused. She even checked the cable was connected at the back, which it was.

"We can't sit here without any communication," moaned Greg. "What if something happens?"

"What are we going to do? Leave?" laughed Lydia. "You know we'd need outside patrol to open the door for us."

"We need to do something!"

"Yes, we wait," chuckled Lydia. "When you've been in this job for as long as I have, you'll know things never work properly. That's the Prison Service for you. So sit there and enjoy your kid's picnic. I'm sure we'll be back online soon."

Suddenly the emergency buzzer from Cell 2-14 bleeped, causing both officers to jump mildly in fright.

"Surely not another one moaning about the football," sighed Lydia, as she moved to answer the intercom. "I thought they'd given up with the TV's."

"I've got a mobile phone," said the prisoner abruptly.

"Nice joke," tutted Lydia as she hung up immediately, groaning in annoyance. Because the prisoner had pressed his emergency buzzer, it would continue to ring until she reset it at his cell door.

As expected, thirty seconds later, the buzzer rang again. It scraped at her brain, like sandpaper across her flesh, with its uncomfortable, unnecessarily loud bleeping.

"I'm going to come up and reset this," said Lydia sharply, eyebrow raised. "If you press it again, there'll be consequences. Get me?"

"I'm telling you I've got a phone so you believe what I say next."

Lydia rolled her eyes. "Which is?"

"We're all in danger! Monsters outside!"

"You've been smoking the same stuff as Leroy, have you?"

"I'm being serious! Please listen to me!"

"So am I, I'm coming up now," she said with a sigh, frustrated. "And I meant what I said."

And so, she climbed the stairs, knowing Greg wouldn't. He'd be happy to listen to the buzzer every thirty seconds. Her? After hearing it pressed maliciously for years, it drove her mad. She heard it in her sleep.

She arrived at the cell door and pressed the reset button on a small electronic box outside the cell.

"I can hear your footsteps, come look!" pleaded the prisoner from the thin gap between his door and the wall. "Open the spyhole, look it's my phone! Come see!"

"Okay," laughed Lydia as she started to walk away.

That was until she heard the familiar ringing of an iPhone timer alarming from the cell.

She immediately returned to the cell and opened the rectangular spy hatch on the door. It slid upwards revealing reinforced glass about as large as an A5 notepad. And there, true to his word, was the prisoner showcasing a white iPhone. It was older, generations old actually. But it was an iPhone all the same.

"See, I told you!"

She couldn't open his door, she wasn't allowed to, and yet she couldn't radio for permission either.

"Okay, I'll entertain you," tutted Lydia as she watched the prisoner cautiously. The cell looked bare, no weapons, no weird inventions. He was dressed in only his boxers and flip-flops. Nothing seemed amiss, nothing seemed malicious. And yet it was too odd for her not to doubt something. No prisoner in the history of her working career had ever shown her an illicit phone so willingly.

"What is it?" she asked.

"Monsters!" he said, waving his hands as if saying 'duh!'.

"You'd really risk showing me a phone just to tell me about these imaginary monsters? You know you'll get extra jail time for this."

"What's extra jail time if I'm dead anyway? That's why I'm showing you," he said irritated, continuing to wave his hands around. "To show you how serious I am!"

"Okay, so what have you smoked? Am I going to open this door to see you overdosed in the morning?"

"Fucking hell," screamed the prisoner. "You always think the same don't you? I must be a junkie like everyone else, huh? Look at this!"

He shoved his screen up close to the spy hole so that Lydia could read;

"Monsters Loose! Dinosaurs? Scientist gone mad! STAY INSIDE TONIGHT!"

Lydia was about to comment on the satire of it until she saw the authentic logo and slogan of the local reputable newspaper at the top. She took a second to read the first few lines;

"Numerous creatures, believed to be dinosaurs have escaped from an Aberdeen biological research facility. Three dead pedestrians were found outside the facility, mauled by means no Scottish creature could achieve. A whistleblower was set to be interviewed to provide insights but police suspiciously picked her up. They now have the place surrounded. One local resident who

claims he saw one of the creatures described it as what is commonly known as a velociraptor and another..."

Lydia gave up reading, deciding it to be a joke article or an edit.

"Dinosaurs?" chuckled Lydia. "That's the best you could come up with? That was worth the punishment you'll get for having the phone?"

"My mate from another block was texting me, saying he could hear screaming and growling outside. Now he's not replying back! And I heard you with Leroy! They're here."

"Okay, stay off that buzzer now," replied Lydia, unphased. "Will see you soon for that phone."

"I didn't want to do this," said the prisoner. "But I'm phoning the police."

And then she heard ringing as the phone tried to connect.

"I'm ordering you to hang up right now!" commanded Lydia. She then turned her head over the balcony. "Greg get up here right now!"

"You're the one making me do this!" he screamed.

Lydia turned back to the prisoner. "You'll get in so much bother for this! Just hang up!"

"I don't care, I'm not dying tonight. I'm phoning the police, I'll be phoning everyone I know and they'll be at your gates tonight."

"999, what's your emergency?" said an operator's voice over the phone.

"I need the police, help! I'm in danger!"

"Ah fuck," Lydia said to herself. And against her better judgment, she drew her baton, pulled her cell keys from her pocket and opened the door.

"Give me the fucking phone!" she commanded.

But the prisoner stepped backwards. "Someone's just been killed, send help!" he shouted into the phone. "They're about to kill someone else!"

Lydia swung her baton as quick as a boxer's jab. With great force it smashed into the phone, obliterating it into pieces as it travelled towards the wall.

"Ahh, my fingers! You assaulted me! My fingers!"

Lydia quickly retreated out of the cell, keeping her eyes pinned to the prisoner and her baton raised as she reached for her keys.

She froze, like a stray cat in the night, at the enormously loud thunder exploding throughout the entire block. It was as though the door had been torn down – a gust of wind rushed through, tickling her hair bun. Perhaps the entire wall, given that the whole building shook.

She turned to see Greg next to her, as motionless as her, mouth ajar in fearful anticipation.

"I told you!" screamed the prisoner as he charged out of the cell. He did so with so much force, so much haste, that he pushed Lydia into the barrier and over the edge.

Her fingers grasped at the railing as her body tumbled over. But she failed to find her grip and fell to her demise, through a hole in the netting.

She screamed as her body slammed into the ground, headfirst, with a deafening crunch.

"Ughhr erghhh," she spluttered in shock.

She lay there, twisted and broken like tangled wire; head stuck facing the door. Bone protruded past her left knee. Both her right arm and right foot bent opposite how they were supposed to. And bloodshot claimed one of her eyes, the white of such no more; replaced entirely by dark crimson as it created a flow of red tears falling down her helpless face.

"Help, please..." she muttered finding words through the thick blood filling her mouth. She wasn't in pain. She could feel... no, she couldn't feel anything. Nothing at all from her neck down. Not even the feeling of the ground against her body. Or the cold against her skin.

But she could see. Although hazy in one eye, her bloodshot one, she could see nonetheless.

She could see a monster of unimaginable horror walk into the open space with menacing prowess. She could see the remains of the door, and surrounding wall, shattered beneath its heavy feet. She could see its enormous scaley body; emerald in colour splattered with blood from its victims. Claws as sharp as a wolf's cunning protruded from its fiend-like fingers. Teeth as deadly as a crocodile's embrace hung from its open jaws, on both of its heads - *both* - because it had two. Two enormous t-rex-like heads sat upon muscly necks like trophies. It was undoubtedly Lucifer's right-hand demon if not the dark lord himself.

Another tear fell down her face as she awaited the inevitable. As she waited for the demon to end her life.

But it didn't, not right away.

Because its hunting instinct, the villainous evil inside it, opted for the live hunt first. She couldn't see what it did next. Her head couldn't turn, victim to her broken spine.

But as the creature escaped her vision, she could hear the screams of Greg. His agonising screams. The prisoner's too. She could hear squelching. Chomping. Chewing. Squealing. She could hear dozens of different noises as the creature clawed and munched its way through its prey. And the screams continued. The howls. Longer than she expected. As if it was playing with them, rather than mercy killing. As if it was enjoying every second, every slash, every bite, taking pleasure in the hunt.

And all she could do was listen and sob some more.

She closed her eyes, and yet that seemed so much worse. Being trapped in the darkness. The blind unknown. The waiting. And so, she'd face her death if she must, she decided.

Seconds dragged on like infinite hours. She willed every fibre of her being to move. She begged. And begged. And begged. And begged. She wasn't religious but she even reached out to God, pleading for his protection. Begging and begging and begging. To give her strength. To let her move her body once more so she could run to safety. To spare her.

She willed with everything she could. She willed every thought into her legs. But it only led to frustration. Because nothing moved. Not even an inch. Not even a centimetre.

And then she felt it. A drop. A warm drop on her cheek. Another. And another.

A snarl.

A growl.

A further drop fell into her eyes causing her to blink rapidly. Her vision turned red in both eyes. Was it blood? The blood of another human dripping onto her face? Into her eye? The thought disgusted her to her very core and yet she couldn't wipe it away. She was as helpless as ice on the sun.

Her vision spun violently as she was lifted into the air and forcibly thrown across the block.

Her loose neck nearly turned full circle before muscles whiplashed her head back into place. She landed with a loud thump. And when she did land. She had the privilege of watching the creature tear into her abdomen with both heads.

It was a blessing that she couldn't feel as she watched her entrails hang from both mouths of the creature. As she watched the cruel smiles on its hideous faces. As she watched the evilness in its monstrous eyes. As she watched the vile... her eyes were becoming too heavy to keep open...

"Lilly? Is that you my beautiful daughter?" she mumbled. Is that...Is that..."

... Blackness.

CHAPTER 8
TWO LOST LOVERS

B ruce blinked his heavy eyelids.

He grumbled in both confusion and pain. He felt groggy, his thoughts messy. His left arm burned as though it melted underneath the hottest blaze. As if Cain's dagger cut through it. Not just his arm though, his entire body felt aflame – sweat poured from his brow.

"Oh thank God, you're alive," muttered Myla gleefully. She stood near a window, keeping guard.

"I a-am?" he mumbled. He swayed his head from side to side as though he was drunk. "I don't feel like it."

He turned his gaze to the inferno claiming his arm. Or rather, the stump from where it had once been.

It had been tied tightly with his shirt to halt the bleeding, leaving his hairy chest and belly exposed. His jacket sat across his right side, like a blanket, providing a little warmth. His heart palpitated as his eyes soaked in the injury. Dread consumed him and he cried out, remembering what had happened. Remembering the torments awaiting to claim his soul – the dinosaurs who'd already tasted his sweet flesh. The dinosaurs who'd eventually taste the rest.

Suddenly he started clambering at the carpet around him, trying to crawl away. Anywhere and yet nowhere.

"Bruce," whispered Myla as she rushed over and grabbed his other hand, his only hand. "It's okay, I'm here. You're safe."

But Bruce didn't feel safe. Tears ran down his face. His heart beat rapidly. What a nightmare, he thought. What a nightmare! What a nightmare! What a nightmare!

"I want to go home, Myla. I just want to go home. Please take me home. I'm so scared."

"We will," she reassured, wiping sweat from his face. "We're going to go home, okay?"

"It's too much Myla," he cried. "It's too much. I want to keep you safe but I'm so scared. I don't know how to. I don't know how..."

"I know," she said, kissing his forehead. "I'm scared too."

"Where did we go wrong?" he wept. "I still love you, so fucking much. I just, I j-just..."

"You've lost a lot of blood," she awkwardly chuckled. "You're delirious you are."

He looked at her with sad eyes. "Tell me you don't feel the same. I know we lost our way. But were we wrong in ending things? I just want to hold your hand and call you mine again."

"Bruce," she said as her own eyes welled up. "We gave it our best shot, now isn't the time for this."

"Then tell me you don't love me, that you don't feel the same? That these few months haven't been the worst in your life?"

She looked away.

"It's been four months," he said, sobbing. "And you're all I can think about. You're all that I think about."

"Oh Bruce," she sighed, pulling him into an embrace as he passed out once more.

When Bruce regained consciousness, he felt sick, dizzy and lethargic. His pained body was still victim to the Devil's penance but he felt of sounder mind. The shock of his situation had seemingly worn off and he felt more in control. For now, at least.

"How long have I been out?" he muttered. He noticed Myla had taken off her bomber jacket and wrapped it around him.

"The first time? Fifteen minutes maybe?" said Myla. She was cuddled into him, head on his chest. "The second? A little longer."

"Sorry," he mumbled, as he remembered the conversation they'd just had.

"Don't apologise," she replied with a warm smile. "How about we talk about it after this is all sorted okay?"

"You mean it?" he asked.

"You're not the only one hurting," she said as she sat up. "Or missing what we had."

He returned a warm smile of his own. "I'd like that."

"Where even are we?" he asked as he also sat up, against the wall, and looked around. They were in a room with plastered walls, desks and stacked chairs. Modern, unlike prison blocks. The door was closed and a mop was forced through the handle to keep it that way. In the corner sat a trolley, used to cart heavy objects between blocks. Blood dripped from it, so he presumed Myla used such to transport him here.

"One of the training classrooms, not too far from Charlie Block. I couldn't haul your fat arse much further."

Bruce looked at his missing limb. "I should be a little lighter now?"

She chuckled, but Bruce could see it was out of sympathy. The injury was an indicator of their future, and they both knew it. It signalled the truth that neither wanted to admit. The likelihood that they were both to die here tonight. They could pretend otherwise. They could dream of home, of safe havens. But this was it, their reality. There was no escape. What could they do, what could the two of them do against dinosaurs?

"How did you even get in?" asked Bruce. "Your keys can't open this?"

She shook her head and waved a set in front of his face. "No, but yours can. Those prisoners didn't last too long out there. I picked these off Pascal's corpse on the way. I'd say it was pretty lucky."

"Lucky," scoffed Bruce as he stared at his stump.

"Oh no, I didn't mean -"

Bruce sighed. "Thank you." He sulked forwards staring at the carpet and gave thanks again.

"What do you mean? I wasn't going to leave you out there, silly goose!"

"I don't mean that, well aye I do. Thank you," he said. "But I mean for staying. Here, now. Those things could have come back at any second, and you stayed. They still might."

She shrugged. "I figured it's safer in here with you. After all, they'd go for your blubber, not little ole me."

He laughed, causing himself to wince in pain. His side felt bruised from when he was attacked earlier. Nothing hurt as much as his arm though. It pierced his thoughts every other second. He'd never felt anything like it, not even the worst paper cut could compare.

"So what now?" he asked.

Myla pulled the radio from her belt.

Bruce scoffed; he had completely forgotten about the radio.

"Have you tried communicating?" he asked.

"Yes but there was no reply," she said as she passed it over. "You try. If they were talking to Chris then it's maybe a man's voice they're expecting."

He nodded in agreement.

"Hello?" said Bruce, pressing the transmitter. "Anybody there?"

Silence.

"Hello?"

Silence.

"I know you're there!" he shouted, but he was quickly silenced by Myla.

"Shhh," she hushed, looking around the room, half expecting a dinosaur to burst through the wall at any second. "Quieter."

"Please," begged Bruce, almost whispering. "I'm an officer, I need help."

"I told you," sighed Myla. "Nothing."

"Please," sobbed Bruce. "Please help us. Please. We're officers in HMP Kirkwood. We need help. We're injured. It's bad."

Silence.

"I'm begging..." he muttered as he stared at the screen in desperation, praying for a response. "We just want to go home."

A second later, they heard a crackle, a crackle of someone pressing their transmitter.

"Where's your manager Chris, over," came an unfamiliar voice sternly.

Bruce's eyes lit up. This could be it he thought, they might just make it after all.

"Chris..." started Bruce. "Chris didn't make it. I'm Bruce Cooper, I'm the outside patrol."

"I see."

"And I've got another officer here, Myla, from one of the blocks. It was overrun by some giant lizard creature." He neglected to say dinosaur in case they thought he was crazy.

"Hmmm."

"Can you help or not?"

"Can you get to the emergency access gate?" asked the voice. "That's your only shot."

"The what?"

But the silence returned.

"Hello?" asked Bruce.

Silence.

"Hello? Come in?"

Silence.

He looked at the display and saw four bars of signal. He was still connected to their frequency. They could hear him, and yet they were choosing not to reply.

Bruce threw the radio at the wall in frustration.

"The emergency access gate?" he queried.

Myla nodded. "I know where it is, and so do you, you goose. It's the gate at the back of the prison to let ambulances or other emergency services in if the main vehicle lock gets jammed, remember?"

Bruce's eyes lit up. "Oh, *that* gate."

"It sounds like there's help there."

Bruce was silent for a minute. "Maybe. But he didn't sound too helpful. We'd need keys for there too, it was definitely locked when I checked earlier."

"We should still go. They wouldn't tell us to go if we needed the keys. It must be open. Maybe Chris opened it after you'd checked? Or at least there's people there."

"It feels safer in here, with you," said Bruce. He grabbed her hand and squeezed. "Let's just stay here, together."

"And yet why don't I feel safe Bruce?" replied Myla, as she pulled away from his grip. "We have to go."

He didn't feel safe either, not in truth. All he knew was if he were to die here tonight, he wanted to spend as much time with Myla as he could. But she was right, they had to move.

He picked up his heavy body into a stand, using the wall to support himself. The white shirt wrapped around his stump was nearly red in entirety.

Suddenly, the ugly monstrous head of a dinosaur smashed through the window giving both a fright.

Bruce lost balance and fell to the floor. He instinctively placed out his hands to break his fall, landing on his stump instead. His weight collapsed into the tender skin and caused him to cry out, reigniting the agony tenfold. For a few seconds, Bruce was blinded in white pain. His entire body tensed as he tried to push through, incapacitated and helpless.

When he finally managed to come to his senses, fighting every fibre of his being not to fall unconscious, he stared at the uninvited guest.

Stared.

Because he was still alive, so was Myla. In those seconds of vulnerability, he expected his death. And it didn't come, so he stared in both surprise and confusion.

This dinosaur was yellow-brown, boasting slimy scales which reflected the moonlight. The head was petite compared to the others they'd seen, and yet still as ferocious looking. It boasted a shorter snout with just as many rows of jagged teeth. Obsidian black eyes that spoke only the words 'kill' and 'slaughter' sat underneath a large marble-like dome that could break entire countries in two.

It opened its powerhouse of a jaw, attempting to roar once more.

Instead, it choked and let out a deflated gargle. As Bruce and Myla continued to stare, they saw a yellow liquid escape its mouth which they soon realised was blood. The same liquid seeped onto the windowsill and down the wall in copious amounts.

Bruce stood and, daring not get too close to the snapping jaws, looked slightly to the left of the creature. There were large pieces of glass dug deep into its throat. So deep the dinosaur could not retract its head. It couldn't do anything, except suffer as death took hold.

And so, it continued to snarl, but quieter. In pain, rather than intimidation. Its eyes lost their menace and turned vulnerable. For a brief second, Bruce extended a shred of pity before Chris' slaughtered corpse cut across his mind.

"We should head towards that gate," affirmed Bruce.

"Do you think you could make it?" said Myla, concerned after having watched him fall.

Bruce nodded. He had to. He had no choice. He'd crawl if he had to. He'd make sure Myla got there, whatever it took.

"Then let's go," said Myla.

CHAPTER 9
SMALL BUT DEADLY

"We should make a run for it," suggested Bruce as Myla removed the mop and he burst open the door.

And they did, both of them, hands interlocked as Myla took lead, pulling Bruce forwards.

They weren't running from anything in particular. But the reptile's squeaks would bring vicious visitors that neither wanted to wait for. Companions who might blame them for their sibling's death; a wrath they'd rather not suffer.

"This way!" shouted Myla, as she turned left.

Bruce followed, hand still gripped onto Myla's fingers. It helped being ushered as he found it difficult to keep up. He'd lost so much blood, so much energy. Even running with his jacket zipped, tucking in his left stump, was tough to manoeuvre. He felt like a worm as he propelled forwards. He wanted to eat a poisoned apple and sleep indefinitely. Turn off and charge for the next few decades. But burning within him was his desire to protect Myla. Just feeling her skin against his... it's all he ever wanted. And so he pushed his legs to their limits letting that spark ignite him, letting that ambition power his body.

Another left. A right. Forwards. Right again.

They ran between buildings, rows of them. They weren't like the spooky bricked cages which held prisoners. No, these admin and training buildings were built after, losing the Victorian magic.

They were single-storied like the classroom they had sheltered in and resembled something close to both a military barrack and a portacabin. Black horizontal roofs made from steel sat atop frail brick buildings. Crosshatched wire covered glass windows, or *most* of them, as every third or fourth had fallen off – victim to harsh weather over the years.

"Shit," said Myla, stopping and analysing her surroundings.

"What?" replied Bruce as he bowed, appreciating the second to catch his breath. He slumped against the wall of the kitchen building, breathing in thick oily grease that still clung to the air from the earlier gruel.

"It's so dark, I think I'm lost," she whispered, still thinking.

It *was* dark. Like Death herself wrapped her cloak around the entire prison. The fog had returned too, minimising the little light available.

"If that's the kitchen," she said, thinking. "Then that's the recycling workshed and that means we have to go this way between -"

ROAAAAAAAAAAAAAAR!

The dinosaur's cry sounded far away, but it was enough to remind them that time was of the essence. They had to keep moving.

"Go, go!" said Bruce as he lifted himself from the building.

"Where?! I'm lost, I'm lost," panicked Myla as her feet itched to move but her body remained in place. "I don't know, I don't know!"

Bruce could see that she was stressed. He placed his hand on her shoulder to comfort her. "You're right," he said as calmly as he could, trying to appear relaxed and focused. Or as much as he could feign.

He looked at the recycling work shed - a warehouse-type building where prisoners worked during the day sorting through rubbish. He then had an idea. "You were right, you had it. That's the way to the gate. But if we go this way instead," he said pointing, "we will reach the kit store."

Her eyes lit up. She could tell what he was thinking.

"We could get riot gear," he suggested. "Armour. Shields. There'll be some heavy-duty batons in there. They could do some damage I bet."

"Your arm though," said Myla. "You need a hospital. We can't afford to."

"Then we should quit talking and go before whatever roared -"

Myla shook her head and interrupted him. "We can't afford to, Bruce."

"That gate is at least another five minutes away. Longer if we have to detour. And what if we're stopped by a dino? If we get a little armour, we might push through. That might be what helps us make it."

They didn't have time to debate any longer.

Time had run out.

They hadn't seen them
until it was too late.

Masked by fog, nine silent assassins had followed the scent of Bruce's blood.

They appeared from the haze as a group, all nine of them, exposing their teeth like rabid dogs. The brown lizards were only around a foot tall but each of their jaws were as long as an alligator's. It was disproportionate to their skinny bodies and still, they stood tall, balanced by their lengthy, meaty tails.

Both officers ran for the kit store, both thinking the same – shelter. Of course, they could have run into the kitchen, recycling workshed, or any of the closer buildings. But that would have taken time. They needed distance before fumbling keys through a locked door.

Yet that distance didn't come easy.

Despite their petite legs, the creatures moved as fast as sharks in water. Their tails slapped at the ground as they ran, pushing them forwards. And so, as both officers moved in full sprint, quicker than they'd ever run before - the creatures kept up. One even found the strength to turn its momentum into a jump. It threw itself through the air like a biological missile, only narrowly missing Bruce's head with its massive jaw.

"Run ahead," screamed Bruce, quickly tiring. He knew he wouldn't be able to keep up this pace. "Get the door to the store open!"

Bruce turned, took a deep breath, and stood his ground, preparing to face the snapping fiends. He instinctively grabbed at his baton with his left hand. Of course, even if he had a left hand anymore, he no longer had a baton.

'Shit,' he thought, forgetting it had shattered.

The first dinosaur was quickly upon him and like a gymnast, it jumped through the air towards Bruce's throat. He managed to swipe it away, almost catching his fingers between its pointed whites.

Distracted, he wasn't able to stop a second gremlin from wrapping its jaw around his calf. Its teeth were small but nonetheless sharp. They pierced through his trousers, his skin and even into his muscles, almost causing him to fall.

Bruce kicked his leg into the air and although he lifted the dinosaur along with it, the creature stayed firm with its python grip. Its claws swiped furiously, both its arms and legs, ripping fabric to shreds as it sought the skin underneath.

"Bruce! It's open," he heard Myla shout.

"I'm occupied," screamed Bruce as he patted away another creature attempting to find ecstasy within his throat. He was beginning to feel overwhelmed, like a hen in a fox den.

He frantically stomped his leg, attempting to free his flesh from the grip of the beast. Up and down, up and down, he slammed his foot against the ground with all his might.

The dinosaur held strong still, but the others stopped attacking so hastily at least. They analysed his movements, looking for an opening between his erratic dancing. They circled him, looking for his flank.

Now surrounded, he was forced to spin in circles swiftly, lest he end up with a new dinosaur necklace around his neck.

Suddenly he winced and stumbled forwards. The teeth chewing his leg dug even deeper – the strength of the creature's jaw crunched at his muscles, threatening to turn them to mince. Despite the pain, he caught his balance – narrowly – causing an adrenaline rush to wash over him. Another stumble, and it might be his last.

Afraid and panicking, Bruce tried punching the beast - to no effect. Its grip only tightened like an executioner's noose.

That was until its skull shattered under the wrath of Myla's baton.

She'd raced forth to save Bruce, swiping at the creatures and breaking their formation.

"Come on," she insisted as she pulled Bruce towards the door.

She then pushed him ahead and faced the creatures herself, continuing to swing her baton through the air in a criss-cross motion to keep them at bay. She moved backwards, holding each creature in sight.

Once she'd made it to the kit store's entrance, Bruce grabbed her shoulder and pulled her in. She slammed the door shut and swiftly locked it.

"You found the key quick!" praised Bruce.

Myla sucked at the metallic taste upon her lips. It was as uncomfortable as a fork scratching against a plate. "I sucked the key with my spit so I could find it easier."

"Thank fuck for that," breathed Bruce heavily as he looked at his leg. Numerous gushing holes and rugged scratches decorated his skin between the remaining fabric. "I'm not going to make it, am I?"

Myla slapped his face. "You are, okay? You fucking hear me? You better make it!"

Bruce nodded and tried to focus, trying to fight away the negative thoughts.

"Yes, boss!" he said, mocking a salute.

But no matter how hard he tried to fight away his fear, his negativity; reality stung harder than the slap. Because he didn't believe he was going to make it. But he'd pretend, he'd pretend long enough to get Myla to safety.

CHAPTER 10
ARMED AND DANGEROUS

Myla reached for the lights before suddenly stopping herself. "We should maybe keep the lights off."

Bruce nodded in agreement and looked around. Their eyes had already adjusted to the night's harsh darkness, and enough moonlight spilt through the two windows across from them.

On the far left, in premade sets, was body armour of various sizes. Each set, all charcoal black, contained the same; fire-resistant overalls; Kevlar chest, back and shoulder armour; shin, thigh and arm guards; steel boots; thick chainmail gloves; and hardened helmets with sealed visors to defend against thrown liquids.

On the other side of the room were weapons and tools for destroying barricades; shields, metal spears, batons, grappling hooks and even sledgehammers.

"Where should we start?" asked Myla.

"With replacing the shirt wrapped around this," replied Bruce, looking at the lump underneath his bomber. A large wet patch, visible through even the black of his jacket, taunted him; reminding him that with every passing second, death drew closer. Blood also dribbled down his body soaking into his trousers.

To his immediate left was a walk-in shower and stack of towels. "Could you tie this around my arm if possible, please?" he asked Myla as he picked up one of the rough, navy towels and handed it to her.

Myla nodded. "Of course."

Bruce painfully removed his jacket and sat down on a blue bench, revealing a blood-soaked dripping mess hanging from his stump.

Yet as Myla began to tear the ruby shirt away, Bruce had to stop her – almost immediately.

"No," he grimaced, holding back tears. The fabric had glued to his flesh underneath. Removing the shirt, even with Myla's gentle touch, pulled away the tender tissue. "Tie the towel over the top please."

And so she did, round and round, as tight as Bruce would let her. Halfway through, he stopped communicating altogether. The pain was so great, he turned away and bit his lip. When it was done, when Bruce's arm was completely wrapped and tied, he rested it against his thigh.

"You know... this looks like you have a wrecking ball attached to your arm," joked Myla, trying to break the discomfort from Bruce's sniffling face. "If only it was real then those dinosaurs wouldn't mess with us."

"If only," he said softly with a warm smile, only entertaining the humour out of politeness. His pained eyes looked down at a puddle of blood beneath his feet. *His blood.* "But I still think I'd rather my arm back."

"Oh Bruce," said Myla, unable to find the words to comfort him. She kissed his shoulder, walked over to a small white wash basin near the shower, and washed Bruce's blood from her hands. When done, she soaked a flannel and returned to Bruce.

"Let's get you cleaned up?" she asked.

He nodded and wiped away a few more tears.

And so she did, she scrubbed the crusted blood from his naked torso as best she could. She soaked his beard too, letting the chunks of vomit free from their wiry hair prison. It wasn't long before she was on to the fourth flannel, having soaked the others with as much blood as they could absorb.

"Thank you," sniffled Bruce.

"Oh, I didn't do it for you," smiled Myla. "I just couldn't deal with the smell of that sick any longer."

Bruce laughed this time. His eyes were still burdened but he appreciated the humour. "You know, I was saving that for later."

"Yuck Bruce," said Myla with disgust. She scrunched her face and gagged at the thought before breaking into her own smile. "The beard's a good look on you though, vomit aside. You should keep it."

"I did always say I wanted to grow it longer," said Bruce. He stroked the wet hairs, twirling them between his fingers. "I kind of got lazy after the breakup. Lost myself a bit."

"Oh," said Myla awkwardly. "So, what are you thinking?" she asked, quickly changing the subject. "Where should we start, what should we take? Full kit?"

Bruce had been thinking about such the entire time. He took one last glance around the room, confirming his conviction.

"I think we should take chest and back armour definitely. And also overalls, arm guards and a helmet. Leave the rest."

"Really?" questioned Myla. "Not even steel boots?"

"Too much and we'll slow ourselves down. This kit isn't meant for running in, remember. Not for long sprints anyway."

Myla nodded in agreement. "True. And weapons?" she asked. "We should take something for fighting with."

Bruce stood and limped over to the other side of the room. Every step forced his muscles to ignite his wounds, electrifying his agony. He had to stop halfway and take a deep breath before continuing.

When he reached the tools, he picked a long grey spear from the wall. The metal was hollow - lightweight - and yet still durable. At around six feet in length, it boasted a sharp pike at one end and a hook on the other for grappling.

"This could do heaps of damage."

"Agreed," replied Myla. "But you're right about choosing practical things we could run with, and I doubt we could with that. Not for very long anyway."

Myla then joined Bruce and peeled a clear circular shield from the wall. She placed her arm through the straps on the inner side. "We should use these arm shields instead of the full-sized riot ones."

Bruce nodded as he returned the spear to the wall. He'd thought the same. Although the Spartan duplicates were small, they would fare better for moving around. The alternative - a six-foot rectangular shield - was as strong as a castle wall and would protect their entire body. But it was considerably heavier and required both arms to use; a privilege he no longer had the luxury of.

"There's the real winner," declared Bruce as his eyes darted towards a row of batons decorating the wall like golden trophies. These were not like the ones they were issued, far from. Made from titanium, these would not shatter so easily. They were thicker and double in length. A dinosaur killer no doubt. Or so Bruce hoped.

"I hear you," said Myla, "and I respect your choice, but I raise you this," she said as she lifted a thick metal sledgehammer into the air with both hands. The red weapon looked cartoonish compared to her petite frame. "I'd love to take this if it didn't require two hands to swing."

Bruce chuckled. "Remember the time at the carnival when you tried the hammer game?"

"It was rigged."

"So that's why you smacked your own foot, huh?"

They laughed together.

"That was a good day," said Myla. "Apart from breaking my toe."

"That's still the best hot dog I've ever had!"

"Shhhhh," suddenly whispered Myla. She pointed towards the window, still clutching onto the hammer.

A silhouette moved outside covering nearly the entirety of both windows. It brought instant darkness to the room blocking most moonlight. And from the little that remained, it recreated the creature's hideous form upon the floor in front of them, if not uglier.

Perhaps it was the way in which the shadows bounced off the rubber floor, but the creature's shape was rugged and spiky. Its distortion appeared like that of a Shinigami and for a brief second, Bruce believed the shadow itself was a monster. That it was going to climb from the ground, seep into his body and wear his skin for the terrified shell that it was.

And the more he stared, the more it moved. Absorbing every fraction of light in the room. Every piece of life as it shapeshifted, as it ate at his and Myla's energy. And for every second it ate, for every second that they grew closer to death, it gained marginally stronger. And the stronger it got, the more terrifying it got. Two arms became three. One tail became four. It wasn't a dinosaur anymore, but something else. Something even more horrifying.

Both officers fell silent apart from their laboured, frightened breathing. They'd gotten so distracted by each other's silliness that they'd forgotten, in those brief seconds, the terror outside.

CRASH!

The hammer fell from Myla's fearful fingers, barely missing their toes. It created a deafening clunk that echoed throughout the kit store.

Both hearts stopped.

And

so

did

the

creature.

The shadow remained still, inspecting the noise, inspecting the air outside, determining if it was the consequence of a worthy meal or not.

Teeth suddenly filled the room. Two feet each in length as the dinosaur pressed its face against one of the windows, casting shadows of the flesh munchers.

Both officers stared at the other in nervous anticipation. They were inches from each other's faces. Bruce could see the very veins on Myla's beautiful eyes. He could see the little scar above her right cheek from a camping trip they'd been six years prior. He could see every detail of her Nordic neck tattoos. He could see every inch that made Myla who she was, every inch that he loved.

They stared into each other's eyes, listening to the other's heart finally beat having been frozen for too long.

As frozen as the shadow that still hovered over the room, that still threatened to kill them on the spot.

Each officer raised their hand at the same time, touching the other's chest where their heart would be.

And despite everything, despite their hairs standing still, despite the fear mauling at their brain...

Both smiled.

Because if they were to die, then both suddenly realised that this was as worthy a moment as any. No words were needed. Because their eyes said enough, their eyes said everything.

And they stayed that way until the light returned to the room, until the shadow had moved for its next victim, and they were convinced they were safe.

"We should head for the gate already," said Bruce.

And moments later, they were dressed in their protective garments. They would have been unrecognisable from each other if not for the lack of Bruce's arm and the scraggly ginger hairs spilling from the bottom of his helmet. Myla had tied a knot in Bruce's overalls which held the towel nicely in place, acting as a further layer to curb the bleeding.

"Shall we?" said Bruce reluctantly.

Myla wrapped her hand around Bruce's right and nodded.

"As ready as I'll ever be," she said.

"Fancy pizza after all this is done?" joked Bruce.

She laughed. "We better hurry then."

CHAPTER 11
A DANCE WITH HADES

Myla opened the door cautiously and closed it just as quietly. Both officers moved swiftly, trying to silence their footsteps as much as they could. Yet every step suddenly felt louder than usual; every crunch of gravel was a deafening earthquake, exaggerated by their lingering fear. Because despite the armour covering them both, they felt exposed – live bait for the shadow monster to return at any moment.

As they turned the corner, away from the kit store and towards an office building, they saw the jail cat surrounded by the army of ferocious miniatures – eight of, Myla having killed one.

"Shit," muttered Bruce, annoyed. He'd hoped they'd have disappeared by now.

Like hyenas, they circled the feline looking for an opening. And although the cat was quick, it was not fast enough to block every attack.

Each tiny lizard took turns scratching the cat's fluff – soft and agile - like sucker punches, weakening its composure as they looked for the kill. And even when the cat returned a swift scratch of its own, it did little to pierce the scaly protection of the creatures.

"We need to go," whispered Myla.

Bruce's breathing suddenly became harder, more demanding, and his vision flickered briefly. A bout of dizziness washed over him as he struggled to swallow the air around him. It felt impossibly thick. And the more he gasped, the tighter his throat squeezed and the heavier the air felt.

Was it fear? Was it the sudden realisation that no matter what they did, death was inevitable? Was his body finally shutting down, giving up? Were his injuries finally enough to invite a reaper to come for his soul? Thoughts flooded his brain, bringing him to a panic. Why were the dinosaurs still here? Why? Why? Why? How was he to escape with his leg the way it was? How was he to keep Myla safe? How? How? How?

"I n-need a moment," he panted, clutching his chest.

"What's up?" whispered Myla as she pushed Bruce back into the cover of the building in case one of the dinosaurs turned.

"No energy," he groaned breathlessly. He perched himself against the wall of the kit store. "C-can't go on, need a s-second."

"It's just a panic attack, you're okay," assured Myla. She lifted his helmet's visor and then grabbed his hand. "You used to get these all the time, remember? Count backwards, deep breaths. Ten, nine, eight..."

"My arm, it's so sore, I can't go on. My leg. My ribs. I'm so tired."

"Bruce, I'm sorry, but we need to go, you have to count backwards," she said anxiously. She peered her head around the building and watched one of the dinosaurs sink its long jaw around the neck of the cat, silencing its hisses. The rest then pounced on top, tearing flesh from its body like a king would a boar at a banquet. It wouldn't be long before that meal was gone and they'd be looking for another.

"Y-you go," said Bruce, trying to focus. He concentrated on Myla holding his hand - he soaked in her touch, trying to fight away the panic. "I'll follow when I can."

"Breathe with me Bruce," said Myla. "In and out, in and out."

And he did, he breathed with her.

Just like she said,

In and out,

in and out,

in and out.

"Good, keep going."

In and out,

in and out,

in and out.

It helped slow down his thoughts, it helped lighten the air around him.

In and out,

in and out.

Yes, he could suck in the air now, he could calm the storm racing through his brain.

He still felt exhausted but at least breath was finding its way through his lungs once more. At least his thoughts were his once more.

A roar like a hurricane's whistle attacked their eardrums. Powerful, demanding – far from any croak the small dinosaurs could make. Whatever made it, spooked all eight terrors. Each scattered like rats, abandoning their prize.

It was also enough for Bruce's drained legs to find life once more. Exhausted or not, injured or not, adrenaline surged through him and his legs broke into a run. He grabbed Myla by the arm and pulled her along.

"That sounded close," panted Myla.

"Too close," agreed Bruce, trying to focus, to keep his momentum. He concentrated on every detail, every brick he could see, every piece of rubbish, everything and anything to stop the dizziness from washing over him again. He had to remain present.

They'd only sprinted for around two minutes before another roar echoed between a set of buildings they'd found themselves between. It was a roar from the same creature as before, frightening as ever. Like Hell itself was opening and screaming at them.

They stopped to find their bearings.

"I can't tell if we're heading towards it or if it's behind us," said Myla, terrified.

They stood at a crossroads of sorts, with buildings all around them: all different types of worksheds; paint sheds, woodwork, and laundry. These buildings were taller and seemed to steal the moon, casting them into a demonic shadow.

The wind amplified the monster's cries, filtering them between the buildings. They came from all directions. Bruce and Myla stood back-to-back, turning in circles. Eyes were pried open at every route, every opening.

They dared not blink.

Hearts beat faster,

and faster,

and faster,

and faster.

Neither knew hearts could beat so fast. It was as though their hearts were as petrified as their hosts. As if they were trying to burst from their chests, to explode their way to freedom.

"Should we keep running?" asked Myla. "These are the last few sets of buildings before the final push for the gate."

"I don't know," admitted Bruce, as terror threatened to freeze him still. His entire body shook and yet his legs remained stationary.

And then Bruce saw it.

He wished he hadn't.

He wished it was imaginary.

But it wasn't, causing his racing heart to plummet to the depths of the Abyss below; a scout for his soul which would inevitably follow.

Because this was it,

this was his end.

No man could beat the creature in front of him.

This. Was. His. End.

This was a two-headed beast of indescribable nature: Satan himself.

Because if these dinosaurs were birthed from darkness - if they were from Hell, then this was their king. This was the devil itself. This was Hades. This was Hel. This was Osiris. This was every dark deity ruled into one hideous, monstrous abomination.

Every step the green creature took was dreadfully frightening; heavy footsteps like bangs from funeral bells. Talons clicked against concrete, scratching at the gravel, teasing the torture to come - like the noise Death would surely make approaching her kill.

He could feel Myla turn around. And although he couldn't hear it, he knew she was screaming. He knew that the silence from her gasping mouth spoke more terror than any volume; he knew no amount of pitch could quantify the monstrosity in front of them.

It moved slowly, eyeing both officers suspiciously. It could smell their blood, their fear, their human flesh. And yet not a flicker of human skin was in sight. And that seemed to throw it off, enough that it didn't attack immediately. It was cautious, analysing; demonstrating that it possessed intelligence.

"You run to safety," whispered Bruce. "Keep running behind us, through the row of buildings with bins to the left, you'll see the wall, follow it to the gate."

"Not leaving without you."

"I'm done for," said Bruce as he watched the demon halt. It was around eighty meters from them. "I'm barely alive. My leg, I don't think I can go on. I'm lucky I've ran so far. But you, you have a chance."

The creature raised its enormous heads and like a lion roaring to claim its birthright, it roared from both mouths simultaneously. It was deafening, like a banshee's wail. The roars echoed off each other, amplifying the menacing howls to an unbearable level. If it wasn't for his thick helmet, Bruce was sure his eardrums would have exploded.

"Rooaaaaaaaaaar," imitated Bruce as loud as he could, before fear turned his voice high and he broke into a cough.

"What are you doing?" said Myla in astonishment.

"I-I-I don't know," admitted Bruce as he coughed again to clear his throat. "I don't know."

He didn't know. Out of options, perhaps out of quickly fading sanity, his brain fumbled. He didn't even think, he'd just acted. Out of stupidity to most, and yet survival to him.

One head of the creature snarled and the other growled. Their vocals were like laughter, as though they were entertained by Bruce's feeble show of strength.

No longer considering the duo a threat, the creature charged with all its deathly might.

Despite powerful legs driving it forward in quick haste, its bulky muscles were slower than the other dinosaurs they had encountered. It was enough time for Bruce to unclip the enforced baton from his chest armour, extend it, and bring it behind his head, ready to strike.

When the creature was close,

he swung,

and missed.

His non dominant hand had failed him.

Inches from the creature's head, Bruce's baton sliced past, almost taking himself to the ground with the sheer force he threw into it.

The creature snapped back with its right jaw. The shield around Bruce's arm stopped teeth wrapping around his flesh. Instead, the dino's snout rubbed bloody saliva across the hardened plastic.

The left head howled into the night as the right snapped its jaw once more. This time it wrapped its teeth around the top of the shield, trying to pry it from Bruce's arm. Instead, it lifted Bruce off of his feet.

Using her own shield, Myla pushed into the creature's left side with all her strength.

And yet it didn't budge.

The creature didn't move.

It stood firm, like the machine it was.

Both heads turned their attention to her, releasing Bruce's shield and dropping him to his feet.

In that brief second, before the creature mustered a retaliation, Bruce swung his baton through the air with all and any momentum he could gather. This time - angered by the thought of the creature attacking Myla, Bruce made significant contact with its right skull.

Dazed and surprised, the monster took a few steps backwards. One of its eyes fell, like it was cockeyed, as the head snarled and coughed in pain. A large dent appeared upon its head, splitting the skin, and showcasing broken skull underneath.

Bruce looked at the baton like a samurai would his sword after a great battle. He felt powerful, victorious. The baton was bent slightly, but it was intact. He could use it again if he needed to. And some hopeful part, some naivety perhaps, told him he wouldn't have to. As he watched the creature continue to back away, yellow blood drowning its face, he dared feel this was a battle won.

"Come on," ushered Myla as they both turned and ran as fast as they could, breaking into a final sprint.

Heavy footsteps pounded behind them.

Faster and louder, like a percussion orchestra reaching climax.

Bruce didn't want to turn, he didn't want to see the creature chasing them. Not when they were this close to the gate, this close to safety. He hoped with every fibre of his being that he was imagining the mammoth footsteps, that fear was tickling his imagination once more.

Myla quickened her feet killing his hope.

The creature *was* behind them.

But not for long.

Because out of the corner of Bruce's left eye, he saw the creature to his side, on top of one of the worksheds.

It followed in their direction, leaping to the next building with agility and finesse that shouldn't be possible for a creature of such colossal size.

SMASH!

As it landed upon a fourth building, the aged roof gave way underneath the dinosaur's weight and it fell through - animated by its own roars. The noise was ugly, ear-splitting – a combination of the dinosaur's wails, the crumbling of the building, and the merciless destruction of everything it landed upon inside.

"Faster," panted Bruce. He forced his pained leg to fight through the agony and speed up before the creature could catch him.

Because,

despite falling perhaps ten or twelve feet,

the creature continued its pursuit.

It tore through the brick wall seemingly unphased. It cheered victoriously with an ugly grumble, shaking plaster and mortar from its tough hide before attempting to close the distance that Bruce and Myla had created.

The access gate was in sight, only a few hundred meters away. But Bruce's lungs burned. And his injured leg threatened to give up any and every second. The torn muscle pulled and stretched, begging him to stop. But he couldn't. He wouldn't.

The creature gained quickly, turning its run into a pounce. Millimetres from Bruce's head was the snap of a jaw. It was enough to force his legs beyond their limits. His heart beat every drop of adrenaline his body could muster, putting every resource into this run, a last-ditch effort for survival. This was it, live or die.

A hundred and fifty meters away.

The gate looked open. Maybe only halfway, but it looked irregular all the same. Strange as it was, Bruce was convinced he could see lights. Flashing lights. Blue, red. Like emergency services.

One hundred meters.

Yes, there *were* lights. And voices, the wind was carrying voices towards them.

Seventy-five meters. Everything was in slow motion. Despite the short distance, this felt like the longest run in Bruce's entire life. Every millisecond felt like an entire minute. Every moment that passed, he expected the jaws of the Underworld to wrap around him and lead him to his death. And when it didn't, he presumed the next would. A continuous cycle of carnivorous torture.

"AHHHHHHHHHHHHHHHHHH!"

A scream, a scream that cut through Bruce's heart harder than any dinosaur's teeth ever could.

Despite being ahead by a meter, the monster had lunged forwards and snapped up Myla.

Bruce halted his steps.

"MYLA!"

But it was too late. The creature held her between one of its jaws, suspended in the air. Its teeth cut through her abdomen, spilling her blood over the concrete. It fell in puddles, like a wash basin turned over.

Suddenly, the beast slammed Myla onto the ground with tremendous force and roared its loudest roar yet, like a wolf howling to its pack. A howl from an alpha. It ruled the night, it ruled the prison, and it was letting Bruce know.

And then it grinned. It bore its bloody teeth as its lips curled on both heads, turning into the venomous smiles that ate into Bruce's soul. It was a smile that ruled nightmares, that haunted daydreams. It was so cruel, it absorbed the darkness of the night and turned it to day.

And then the creature stomped its leg into Myla's wound and cut its enormous talons across her body, left to right, spilling her guts. It looked Bruce dead in the eye, as if saying 'watch this', before leaning over Myla, wrapping its left jaw around her leg and tearing it off in one swift, merciless movement.

"Myla," whimpered Bruce as his own heart stopped. "Myla..."

CHAPTER 12
UGLY TRUTH

Bruce had never felt rage like it. It came at him out of nowhere.

"AAAAAAAAAAAARGHHHHHHH!"

He charged, filled with vengeance, drawing on the few remaining embers of energy pumping around his dying body. Until those embers turned into a full blaze.

Suddenly he didn't feel scared, not a flicker of fear touched his bleeding heart. Just anger. Fury. A burning storm that made him feel invincible, that powered his broken body. It strengthened it, as if Gods themselves flooded their might through him, as though he was destined to crush the evil in front.

BANG! BANG!

Gunshots all around him.

BANG! BANG!

BANG!

BANG! BANG! BANG!

He ducked in fright as red lasers from assault rifles showered him. The creature squealed and croaked taking multiple steps backwards as bullets tore through its strong, yet vulnerable frame. It continued to cry out in pain until its wails got dimmer, fading into the night to one final earthquaking bang of its enormous corpse slamming into the ground.

Bruce was confused. Gunshots? Was it hallucinations? The warping of reality as his body shut down and his mind slipped into euphoria? Did the creature really fall to its demise? It didn't matter, to him, not now. Only one thing did. Because even if his mind was playing tricks, one thing remained regretfully true.

He crawled over to Myla.

She already lay in a pool of thick red.

"Myla," he sobbed, "Myla!"

He brought himself to his knees, picked up her hand and stroked her fingers. "Myla..."

She whimpered, recognising the voice. A fragile, weak whimper. "B-Bruce?"

Bruce took off his helmet, then hers, and placed her head gently upon the concrete.

"It's going to be okay," said Bruce, squeezing her fingers.

But he knew that was a lie as he looked upon her dying body.

A deep crater-like gash cut across her abdomen, and even that of the armour, shy of splitting her in two. She was beyond recovery. Her entrails, like parasitic worms looking for a new host, leaped from her wound, across the harsh gravel, soaking in dust and dirt. And then there was her leg, or lack thereof. The stump, shredded and frayed, pumped blood from her body by the literal second. It was mangled, like minced meat, from the sheer viciousness that it was torn off - an impossible task to sew back.

"I'm s-scared," she whispered. Her voice was soft, faded; almost mute as her vocals failed to find the strength to talk.

"I'm here Myla," choked Bruce. Tears flowed freely down his face. "I'm here."

"W-where?" whispered Myla. Her breathing was laboured. "I- I can't see."

Bruce leaned over and kissed her forehead. "I'm right here love. I'm right here."

"I l-love y-you," managed Myla. "I think a-about you every day."

Bruce wailed as the words crushed his heart causing palpitations. "Do you remember when we first met?" he sobbed.

A smile washed over her pained face. "Ice skating."

"I told you then, I told you then that you were the most beautiful girl I'd ever seen, didn't I? I told you that we'd be together till the end, didn't I? And you said," Bruce stopped to laugh as he wiped tears from his face. "You said, why the hell would I want to date a boy who wore skinny jeans? Never mind a boy who wore skinny jeans to ice skating?"

A tear fell from her face as she listened.

"I said if you dated me, I'd never wear them again, didn't I? It was the best decision of my life, you know. I've never worn them again."

Bruce scrunched his face as his tears flowed a waterfall of despair. "I love you so, so fucking much, I'm so sorry. I'm so sorry the way we ended things. We were so silly to do so."

But Myla's face lacked any animation other than the single tear falling to the ground.

"Myla! Myla! No, please, no!"

He grabbed her hand but her limp fingers fell from his grip.

"Myla!" he said, once more, falling into her chest as he wailed into the night.

"We'll take it from here," said a soft voice, as someone touched his shoulder.

But he didn't move, he wouldn't let her go.

"Sir, let us take it from here," said the voice again as he felt himself being pulled from her.

"No, Myla!" he roared.

He turned towards the voice and saw soldiers with medical equipment. Two had a stretcher and instantly placed Myla onto it, lifting her cautiously.

"There's still a pulse, but it's faint, it's not looking good," shouted a female medic. "Get her out of here now!"

"I don't think she's making it," said another medic before noticing the concern on Bruce's face. "Helicopter is on standby; we will get her in the air!"

Regular soldiers also approached.

Everything seemed so fast, so unbelievable. Bruce struggled to process as people buzzed around him. Before he knew it, he had been helped to his feet by soldiers and carried towards the gate, out of the prison.

"Wait," mumbled Bruce. "I can't leave her."

"Let the medics do their thing okay? Follow us."

"Myla..." he whispered.

They walked, and they walked. And they walked some more. Grief grabbed him by the heart and twisted, sending him to infinite mindlessness - a dark pit - as he let the world go by.

Flashbacks cut across his mind, flashbacks of the dinosaur chasing him, of Myla... of Myla being brutally... of Myla...

He cried out, giving fright to those around him, as his heart beat to the noise of numerous sirens blaring their ugly wails. Only then, broken from his trance, did he realise his surroundings.

"What is this?" he mumbled, looking around.

An entire military base has been created upon the grounds outside of the prison. He could see the prison walls with its razor wire hair, the sea – yes it was definitely outside of the prison. Only maybe three or four hundred meters from the gate. And yet, there were soldiers everywhere. Fifty, maybe even sixty. And that's the ones he could see. There were tents. Trucks. Portacabins. Ambulances. Police cars. There was everything anybody would ever need to start a small war.

'How did they get here so quickly?' he thought as he stared in awe.

"We need to get him to hospital, ASAP!" demanded a passing medic who gazed upon Bruce. He had stripes on his shoulders as if he was in charge. "Why's he just sitting there? He's lost an arm for fuck's sake! Anybody can see that! What are you thinking? Who's your boss? I want answers!"

The two soldiers who were sat with Bruce gulped awkwardly in unison, neither having an answer, nor an excuse.

"Well fuck off and be useful," waved the medic, before he gave his attention to Bruce.

"Sir, I need you to look into my eyes," he said as other medics rushed over noticing the commotion.

One brought a portable bed. Another grabbed Bruce's right arm and unstrapped his armour. She then lifted his sleeve, looking for a vein to insert a cannula.

"Sir, I need you to lie on this bed please."

"He's too pale, he's lost too much blood, this will need to be another air ambulance. I can't even see a vein."

"There's another helicopter on standby, radio the hospital ahead, I'm going to need blood at the ready."

"We need blood *now,* it can't wait."

"How are you even awake, Sir?" asked the commanding medic as he shone a torch into Bruce's eye to assess his responsiveness. "Just hang in a little longer. You've done really well so far."

And then Bruce saw him. The scrawny manager. Laughing. Howling with laughter among those he was conversing with.

Bruce like a raging bull only saw red. He broke into a sprint, or as much as his injured leg allowed him, almost pulling one of the paramedics along with.

"Did you know?!" screamed Bruce.

But before the manager could react, he ate the entirety of Bruce's right fist. And then another. Bruce made three punches before two soldiers pulled him away.

The manager only stared in dazed fright, lost for words.

"Did you know..." sobbed Bruce, breaking into tears once more as he fell to his knees unable to find the strength to stand. And a moment later, he fell into blackness entirely.

Three weeks later

Bruce tried to grab water from his hospital bedsit with his left hand before realising it was just a bandaged stump. He sighed and reached over with his other, trying not to stress his broken ribs too much. Three weeks later and he still wasn't used to having only one arm.

He looked at a newspaper on his bedsit placed there by the morning nurse. He picked it up with an enthusiastic curiosity. He'd been waiting on this ever since that dreaded night. It read;

" *"Breaking news – Truth Finally Revealed"*

Last night a meeting with Dan Rawland, Police Chief; Deborah Hew, Governor of HMP Kirkwood; and George Pender, Major in the British Armed Forces: finally revealed the truth of the horrible nightmare that took hold of HMP Kirkwood three weeks ago.

This of course was made possible thanks to public pressure placed upon authorities and the consequent unrest. Coupled with various statements from whistleblowers from Prehistoric Bio-Tech (PBT), hands were forced, and we finally get to share the truth from the ~~monsters,~~ sorry, – Government's very own mouths.

PBT, recently popular for both; curing Alzheimer's; and its breakthrough research in excavating (and animating) cells from historical fossils for medicinal use, - employed a rogue scientist who took his research one step further. One step too far.

Such scientist - Leading Professor William Spence – will be fresh in many readers' minds. Eighteen months ago, he was victim to a violent attack from a notorious, but small-scale Scottish gang. This group of thugs, known as the Pitbulls, murdered his entire family in a vicious robbery. The assailants were imprisoned for only four years each, and all are due to be released in the coming months due to Scottish sentencing law.

Feeling that a great injustice was done, the professor acted on his own accord - unknowingly to the company, or so they claim. Empowered by vengeance, he made a massive advancement with his research. By evolving how he animated residual DNA, the professor managed to recreate, clone and grow - allowing him to produce living creatures.

By paying off a police officer, he managed to obtain the DNA of his family's murderers (from the evidence used to convict them). He built this into the creature's biological makeup, altering their hunting instinct towards that of the offenders. Another source also tells us that the same police officer disclosed private information - the addresses of the offenders. The Professor used this knowledge to obtain access to the offender's houses. He thieved possessions and left a trail of clothes from the laboratory to the prison through numerous routes. Just enough to trigger a scent and excite the creatures.

The Professor's assistant, one of the whistleblowers, who will remain unnamed, soon made authorities aware of his actions once the creatures were released. Whilst the assistant knew that she was enabling the unauthorised use of company property, she did not know for its true purpose. And never expected such monsters would ever be released upon the world. If we are to believe her side of things, she was told that the creature's existence was proof of an ability to recreate organs. (Her brother is currently on the waiting list for a kidney transplant.) Whether naïve or just as guilty, she remains remanded in police custody.

The police raided the facilities the same evening/night the creatures were released, but none remained, nor did the Professor. They did, however, manage to recover a diary, and his hard drive, discovering much of his plan.

With little time to act, authorities deemed it best to allow the prison regime to continue as normal rather than evacuating. Despite numerous data suggesting an attack was imminent, despite the strong conclusion that these beasts were created as weapons - the prison remained unaware. **In a shocking decision**, *as I'm sure everyone would agree,* **nobody was evacuated.**

When authorities were questioned – apparently their decision was based on the lack of capability to track the 'very deadly monsters.' (Side note, these creatures were so deadly that authorities thought it best to allow them loose upon a bunch of unwitting officers and prisoners. Makes sense, right? NOT!"

I quote from Mr. Pender himself, "we couldn't afford to hunt them, not when we knew where they were going. It's all about affordable loss. We needed them inside, we needed the walls around them. We needed some form of control, a cage. We couldn't let them loose within society."

Affordable loss? We've all heard by now the dire recording of a radio message from a survivor - Officer Bruce Cooper - begging for assistance. How could anybody listen to such a plea from another human and sit outside, rifles at the ready, doing nothing? Was he really nothing more than acceptable loss? An officer who already performs a dangerous job for our safety, to protect society, nothing more than affordable loss?

Mr. Pender's rebuttal to this was the existence of the Professor's diary, where he kept track of every beast (and named them). By waiting for the creatures, every creature to enter, they planned to surround the perimeter, begin extermination, and allow none to escape.

Communications were cut to ensure the plan was not foiled. Cameras were looped, and alarms turned off to allow the Nightshift Manager to open the secondary access gate where, and I write this in disbelief – where authorities had placed possessions of the offenders. THEY AIDED THE CREATURES GETTING

IN. Such manager, now deceased, will remain unnamed. But it would appear through admissions of guilt from those involved, that he was unaware of the full details, or the extent of the danger, and that he was paid £100,000 to do what he did.

Deborah Hew, the Governor, claims that she believed staff would be safe locked behind the doors of the blocks they patrolled. Of course, the power of the dinosaurs was far underestimated - she admits - with some having the strength to scale the entire prison wall. And buildings.

It would appear that despite altering the dinosaur's DNA to a single purpose, they were feral creatures at the end of the day. They could not be tamed to a single kill, a single strand of biological instruction. They were territorial beings guided to an area of familiarity. An area where they sought to be Kings and Queens. And unfortunately, the deaths of one hundred and seventeen prisoners, nine prison staff, and fourteen civilians felt that (bodies found between the laboratory and the prison).

Compensation is to be negotiated for all families involved, and it is expected that internal investigations will lead to criminal convictions of the decision makers who felt leaving the unwitting persons of HMP Kirkwood was a safe and justified plan.

Professor William Spence is still at large. Authorities claim that all dinosaurs were accounted for and exterminated. But can we trust them? And with the Professor still at large, could there be more? Tune in for further updates."

Bruce finished reading in utter disbelief. This whole time, this whole time he was bait? He lost his arm for bait? He watched his colleagues get mauled for bait? Myla?... for bait?

He wanted to be angry, but he didn't have the energy for such. And so, he let the newspaper fall to the floor and stared plainly at the early morning TV, letting time pass by.

A nurse knocked on the door before walking in.

"Cornflakes and toast again for breakfast?"

Bruce nodded.

"Would you like it here or in room eight?" she asked with excitement.

"Room eight?" replied Bruce, confused.

The nurse returned a warm smile. "She's awake, Bruce. She's awake."

THE END?

Thank you for reading. I appreciate every single person who reads any of my work. My mission is to get my stories out there, and if you're reading this, I've accomplished my goal.

If you enjoyed, or did not, I'd love for you to leave a review on my Amazon or Goodreads page please. It really helps!

And lastly, if you love horror I have a few tasters below. The first is one of my favourites from "Time to Scream," a collection of twenty-five horror bites (especially enjoyable around a campfire). The second is the first chapter from "The Crow's Vengeance" - a suspense horror that will leave you looking at birds in the night a little differently.

Time to Scream
TRESPASSID

"Get the fuck out of my pool!" shouted Gary Alexander, a man in his fifties.

He'd had more than enough of the college kids dipping their naked bodies into his pool every day. And who'd blame him? He'd spent a fairly large amount of money on it, almost his entire life savings; never mind the upkeep costs. It was the only pool in the entire village. He'd worked hard for it. Why should these dirty vermin reap the benefits? That's how he saw it anyway; their filthy skins ruining his Godly baths.

"Ah, shut up you old fart," laughed one of the boys.

"Yeah, what are you going to do?" teased one of the girls as they all ran away giggling, leaving their empty rubbish to float over the surface.

There were four of them in total. Two boys and two girls, all around nineteen years of age. And for the last six weeks, out of the seven that Gary had owned his pool, they'd soiled his prize. And for the next three weeks, they continued to do so.

Until the day Gary's anger reached tipping point. He was so furious, so enraged that he grabbed one of them by the neck and pushed his head under the water, causing him to splutter and choke.

"If I see you in this pool again," threatened Gary violently, as he continued to hold the boy underneath the surface. "It will be the last thing you do; do you understand?"

"You're drowning him!"

"Maybe he'll learn," hissed Gary as he let go of the boy, letting him retreat with his group.

"Sorry," mumbled one of the girls as all four of them ran away in fear, neglecting to even grab their clothes or belongings.

Weeks passed, and neither dared go near the pool. No, because Gary Alexander was known to be a bit 'off the rails' - a madman of sorts. It was part of the thrill of enjoying his pool; the 'danger.' But now the students realised that such danger was real; Gary *was* a madman, and they'd pushed him too far. They wouldn't risk it. Not anymore.

Until one Friday drinking session led little Callum, the boldest of the four, to suggest they go back.

"No, he made it clear that he'd hurt us."

"I nearly died for fuck's sake Callum," said the other boy sheepishly. "I swear he was going to kill me."

Callum twirled in delight. "Well, you see, I have insider information."

"Like what?"

"Mr. Alexander is on vacation and will be for the next few days."

"So the pool is free?"

Callum nodded.

"Still, I don't like it."

"He warned us. Let's just go to a beer garden."

"Aww come on," insisted Callum. "It's the hottest day of the year, a little pool time would be excellent."

"It does beat pushing past sweaty bodies in a bar," agreed one of the girls.

"Surely he'll have emptied it?"

"Only one way to find out?" said Callum eagerly.

And so, after a little more deliberation, all four of them ventured forth.

They rang the doorbell first to make sure, hiding behind a nearby bush as soon as it was pressed. Nothing. No response. The lights were off too and the house *did* look in darkness. It would appear that Callum's information was correct after all.

And so, straight to the pool they went, gripping their beers and ciders tightly with glee. They pulled off the tarpaulin cover revealing fresh water underneath - to their delight. Five minutes later, they were all joyfully in the centre of the pool bathing in the endorphins it gifted.

"What a life!" said one of the girls as she lay back in the water.

"A beer, a warm day and skinny dipping with friends," said Callum, "can't beat it."

"Even though it's night, it's still bloody warm!"

"It is," said one of the girls, "but is this water getting warmer too?"

"You're being silly."

"No, it's definitely getting warmer."

"Hey, it kind of is, isn't it?"

"Feels nice though."

"Oh but it's getting really warm."

"Owww, I don't like it."

"My cut is bleeding, and stinging."

"Hey, mine too!"

"This water is getting too hot, what's going on?"

"We should go, this isn't normal."

"Wait, I can't move."

"Where's all of this blood coming from?"

"Ahhrrrrrrhh, my skin!"

"I can't move either."

"It's like concrete."

"Everything hurts!"

"Ahhhhrgh!" screamed Callum.

They all looked around to see skin from Callum's arm floating on the surface, as if his arm was a snake shedding its moult. Except it bubbled and sizzled. Blood seeped into the pool in all directions causing his three friends to flinch and wince. They all tried their hardest to reach the ladder in the corner.

"I'm struggling to move!"

But neither could get there, not properly. No matter how hard they tried. They were all frozen. And it wasn't because the water was suddenly solid. No, not at all. But the slightest movement caused their skin to crack, and tear, letting the vicious water sneak in and amplify the pain. And once the water had crept in, once its talons had made haste, their skin followed suit with Callum's. The inferno that engulfed them entrenched them to their torture.

"Help!"

"Helllllllp!"

"Pleeeeeease, I'm sorry!"

One of the students fell under the water, as the pain caused her legs to buckle. It instantly attacked the softness of her eyes. And when she brought her head back up, all that remained on her scarlet, shredded face was two gaping holes like burnt fried eggs - where her eyes had once been.

They all screamed and howled into the night at the horrors before them.

But it couldn't be heard.

Not over the fizzing of their bodies as they themselves diluted into the water. Until their skin peeled off completely. And if they hadn't died by that point, then they felt the privilege of acid attacking their muscles. Until they sizzled into the dark red water, along with their organs, leaving only their bones to float atop.

And once the screaming had subsided, in the darkest corner of the garden, lay Gary Alexander sipping on a cocktail.

"Ah, peace and quiet," he grinned.

Crow's Vengeance
CAWS OF DEATH

August 10th 20.00Hrs

"Anybody fancy a drink?" asked Daryl, as he drunkenly stood from the booth where he and his other four friends sat. There was a look of desperation within his eyes, and a staleness upon his lips, as he itched to reach the bar and fill his belly with another pint.

He *did* have a drinking problem, and today was especially no different. His long ginger hair had been pulled back into a neat bun; but he refused to shave the scruffy, homeless-esque beard dominating his face. Having escaped the suit he had worn earlier, he now dressed in an oddly matched tracksuit; blue jogging bottoms and an ugly red zipper.

"Daryl, you're drinking those pints quicker than a cat does milk," commented Jane judgmentally. "You need to calm down. *Please.*"

"Calm down?" laughed Daryl, as he stared into her viridian eyes. They would, *and did*, steal the gaze of anyone looking upon her beautiful features and flawless hazel hair. "Are you my mother now? My babysitter?"

"No," interrupted Craig as he scratched at his bald head. "She's not. Neither of us are. Which is why we don't want to be the ones carrying you home because you can't stand on your own two feet. Not again, anyway."

"Cut me some slack for fuck's sake," tutted Daryl as he sat back down plainly, trying to hide both his anger and embarrassment. "I know you're only looking out for me, but he was buried eight hours ago. Eight hours, man. I deserve some slack."

Daryl undid his bun and ran his hands through his thick hair, in stressful anguish, as though the world were ending before him. Or as if *his* already had, at least. He then sulked his head, allowing his puffy, tear-exhausted eyes to examine the booth's peeling table.

"I'm just sad, I'm really fucking sad."

"We all are," nodded Sarah with matching grief as she rubbed the dark stormy clouds underneath her own eyes. "Brian was a friend to us all. We all miss him."

"I just can't believe he's gone," sighed Daryl. "He's really fucking gone."

Craig banged his heavy fist against the table. The chunky man, dressed smartly in a black-silk formal shirt and dress trousers, then slammed his fist against his chest. "It's a cliché I know, but he's in here mate," he shouted with absolute conviction before smashing his fist against his chest once more. "And he always will be, just remember that my friend, just remember that."

Sarah shifted closer to Daryl and hugged him tightly. She boasted a cute, innocent persona. Her short brown hair sat just above her neck, and her bangs ever so slightly touched her brows. Large lenses with trendy pink frames clothed most of her face and matched the rest of her indie-style appearance; hoop earrings, denim overalls, and a bright yellow retro t-shirt.

"Craig's right," she said, still gripping him, "as long as we remember him, he lives on, alright?"

"Thanks guys," sobbed Daryl. "It's just–" He paused. "You know I've no family, and Brian, he was my best mate. He was just always there for me. Always."

Sarah laughed politely and slapped his head. "We're your family, you silly goose! We will always have your back. Don't ever think otherwise, alright?"

He looked up at her and smiled pleasantly, and then at his friends who nodded in return; reassuring him that he was not as alone as he felt; reassuring him that the hole in his heart wasn't as gaping as it felt.

"How about one last drink after all?" asked Jane. She fixed herself in her tight blue tube dress and leaned over the table to grab Daryl's hand. "A round of skittle bombs? Brian's favourite. Let's have one to him, grab some good ole grub and then head home?"

"Ugh, I hate skittle bombs," moaned Dillon, the young nerd of the group. He was in his late twenties, like everyone else, but his timid features, and immature style made such hard to believe. His hair was unkempt, and he lacked any real ability to grow a beard. Or any facial hair, really. He sat uncaring in his wrongly sized superhero t-shirt and baggy jeans, scrolling through his phone. And yet despite his perceived rudeness, he was always listening. And his friends knew that.

Jane scowled and pointed her red nails towards him. "It's not about you, Bumfluff. It's for Brian."

Dillon awkwardly sat down his phone, fixed his childish-looking glasses, and stared at Jane apologetically. "Yes, that sounds great," he mumbled, fearing that her intense stare was about to cut right through him.

Sarah stood. "Great idea Jane. I'll go get them then."

Jane laughed and mockingly wiped her forehead. "Well thank goodness for that, Sar. These heels are killing me. I knew I should not have worn them after wearing a pair for the funeral as well."

"That's a cop-out," joked Craig as he gulped the remainder of his pint before slamming the empty glass on the table. "It's your idea so *you* should get them. You can always walk barefoot."

Jane looked around at the run-down pub. The smell of piss and dust and death clung to the air. No, *it was* the air. A stale, murky flavour; far from pleasant and yet familiar enough that they kept coming back.

The booth cushions were burst. The lights flickered. The seats creaked. And the tables were as rough as the actual trees they came from. The only other visitors were old men – regulars like them. The occasional youth group often dared enter but would only ever stay for one drink – if they did not immediately leave, that is.

"In here?" she exclaimed, shocked at the proposal. She even placed a hand on her mouth to imitate that it was the worst idea she'd ever heard. "I would catch the plague no doubt. Anyway. I'd like to see you try and walk in them, but I doubt your fat feet could find a pair that fits."

Craig laughed and gave a wink. "Oh, my good friend, you would never believe what I get up to at the weekend."

"I don't know," chuckled Sarah. "He's managed to squeeze into that shirt that's clearly too small for him."

The group laughed, including Daryl whose smile brought a refreshing colour to his face and an extra grin to the group.

"It really is a shite hole though, isn't it?" agreed Craig as he peeled at the red leather on his seat, showcasing the stained sponge underneath. "Only gotten worse over the years."

"And more expensive," complained Daryl.

"Aye but it's our shite hole and we love it," replied Sarah as she ushered for the others to let her out of the booth. "Five skittle bombs coming right up."

Daryl batted his eyes as her glance caught his. "And a pint?"

"No," she laughed, rolling her eyes. "But nice try."

"What about me?" pleaded Craig. "I'm out of cash until payday."

Jane scoffed. "What on Earth do you spend your money on, Craig? You make double everyone else here."

"Well –"

"Wait!" interrupted Dillon, before Craig could respond, as his eyes ate at something on his phone – something that made his eyes bulge twice in size. "Are you guys seeing this?"

"No, Bumfluff," grinned Craig, as he lightly punched his friend on the arm. "So, show us already."

"Check the group chat," demanded Dillon with urgency. "I've just sent a screenshot from a news article just published."

"An anonymous source claims that Brian Knoll's death might not have been from a wild animal(s) attack after all. Despite numerous unidentified claw marks, the source claims that the actual cause of death was a gunshot wound. The Police

*department has been contacted for further comment due to the compelling evidence that this source brings. We will comment on said evidence pending the department's response. Regardless, we are confident in reporting, at this time, that Brian Knoll was not the victim of a wild animal attack: **he was murdered**."*

Daryl immediately pushed aside his friends, knocking over the glasses on the table, as he rushed out of the booth and darted towards the door.

"Where are you going Daryl," screamed Sarah as she grabbed her bag and jacket, and chased after him.

When she caught up, she instantly banged her hand against the exit door, stopping him from opening it. "Daryl?"

He turned to face her with fire in his eyes, fire that ignited the flame of his hair. His eyes were engulfed with so much emotion, so much anger, that they almost brightened up the dark pub floor.

"I am going to get answers, Sar," he shouted with a raised voice. "I'm going to the police station. If he was murdered, then I want to find the bastard that done it."

"Don't Daryl," she pleaded and grabbed his arm. "You're drunk. You'll get arrested, I know you. You'll say something stupid. Or do something stupid. Just going *is* stupid."

Daryl scrunched his face, turning as red as his hideous zipper. Even the air around him turned to crimson, matching the liquid fury coursing through his veins. "Murdered, Sarah. *Murdered.*"

"You saw him at the funeral home Daryl, he was covered in slashes," she said, shaking her head in disagreement. "*Claw slashes.* You could still see them, even after the undertaker did his best to cover them."

"But it was a gunshot that killed him."

"We didn't see any gunshots, Daryl. That's just the local paper spinning some gossip. You know what they're like. One minute ice cream causes cancer and another; the government is putting breathable trackers in the air. It's clickbait."

"I'll hear that from the police themselves," scoffed Daryl. "The gunshot could have been under his suit; we don't know that. Come on, this is Scotland. When do you hear about deaths from wild animals?"

"And this is Creller town, when do you hear about murders?" she replied sassily.

"Let him go, Sar," Craig said softly, as he and the rest of the group approached behind.

"You want him to get arrested?" spat Sarah in response.

"No, I don't. Of course I don't. But we both know there is no stopping him." Craig then shrugged his shoulders. "And in truth, I'm equally as curious. Wouldn't you want to know how our friend really died? Wouldn't you want to know if he was murdered?"

Sarah looked at him strangely, as if she could see something in his eyes, something that he wasn't telling them. "You know something don't you?"

He stayed silent, keeping his poker face on show.

"Tell me what you know," hissed Sarah, as she grabbed his shoulders. "You always fucking do this lately. You're hiding stuff, I see through your little cover stories. So come on, what do you know?"

"Don't be silly, I know nothing," he lied, brushing off her hands as he turned to the rest of the group. "Now let's go."

Printed in Great Britain
by Amazon

61132505R00078